Milton Friedman

Profiles in
ECONOMICS

Milton Friedman

John Maynard Keynes

Karl Marx

Adam Smith

Profiles in
Economics

Milton Friedman

Cynthia D. Crain and Dwight R. Lee

MORGAN
REYNOLDS
PUBLISHING

Greensboro, NC

Dedication:
In memory of William J. O'Neil,
a champion of free enterprise

Morgan Reynolds Publishing
620 South Elm Street, Suite 387
Greensboro, NC 27406
www.morganreynolds.com
1-800-535-1504

First printing

1 3 5 7 9 8 6 4 2

Library of Congress Cataloging-in-Publication Data

Crain, Cynthia D.
  Profiles in economics : Milton Friedman / by Cynthia D. Crain and Dwight R. Lee.
— 1st ed.
    p. cm. — (Profiles in economics)
  Includes bibliographical references and index.
  ISBN-13: 978-1-59935-108-7
  ISBN-10: 1-59935-108-0
  1. Friedman, Milton, 1912-2006. 2. Economists—United States—Biography. I.
Lee, Dwight R. II. Title.
  HB119.F84C73 2009
  330.15—dc22
  [B]
                                      2009000169

TABLE OF CONTENTS

Early Years

ilton Friedman was the son of immigrants who moved to the United States in the late 1800s. He wrote, "When they arrived, they did not find streets paved with gold; they did not find an easy life. They did find freedom and an opportunity to make the most of their talents." This freedom and opportunity attracted other immigrants to America. And the nation grew and prospered, benefiting the immigrants and their children. Friedman was a child who benefited. He worked hard and took advantage of the opportunities America offered. He took his education seriously and earned a scholarship to attend college.

In the 1940s and 1950s, Friedman became concerned that the nation was losing some of its freedom and opportunity. He believed democratic capitalism was under attack; government control and regulation of the economy were on the rise. Freedom was being buried under an increasing number of government policies enacted to protect and take care of people and control the economy.

Thus, Friedman set out to convince economists and politicians that many of these policies retarded economic

Milton Friedman was one of the most influential economists of the twentieth century. Throughout his long career, he championed the benefits of free markets.

growth and harmed the very people they were supposed to help. In the 1960s, there were few champions of capitalism and free-market economics. Friedman was almost alone in many of his views during the first half of his career. But the power of his arguments and empirical findings began convincing more and more of his fellow economists that his free-market views were correct. Convincing politicians was not as easy, however, so he took his message to the public through popular books and television, and by the 1970s had become renowned as one of the most famous and influential economists in the twentieth century.

Milton Friedman was born at home in Brooklyn, New York, on July 31, 1912, to Jeno Saul and Sarah Ethel Landau Friedman. Jeno had immigrated to America at the age of sixteen from the Hungarian part of the Austro-Hungarian Empire (now known as Poland). Sarah, who grew up in the same country as Jeno although the two did not know one another, had sailed across the Atlantic Ocean at the age of fourteen and joined an older sister living in Brooklyn.

Sarah and Jeno arrived in the United States speaking Hungarian and Yiddish, and had to quickly learn English. They worked long hours at menial jobs, lived frugally, and saved their money. After the two had met and married, they had three daughters—Tillie, Helen, and Ruth. When their last child and only son, Milton, was born, Jeno was thirty-four and Sarah thirty-one.

The Friedman family moved to Rahway, New Jersey, a town of 15,000 people when Milton was one. Jeno, along with many of Rahway's mostly lower-income working-class residents, commuted by train to work in New York City, twenty miles away. He worked as a petty trader or jobber, taking whatever job he could find. He often worked as a middleman, buying merchandise from manufacturers and then selling it to retailers, speculating that he could sell it at a higher price and make a profit on each deal. Sometimes he made money and sometimes he lost money, thus his earnings fluctuated significantly. Even though the Friedmans struggled financially, they managed to earn and save enough money to buy a small building that served as both home and business. Sarah ran the business—a dry goods store—which generated most of the family's income and kept food on the table.

This photograph of Main Street in Rahway, looking south, was taken before 1920. This is the view that the Friedman family would have had from their home, which was located a half-block north of this scene.

Main St., Rahway, N. J.

Another view of Main Street in Rahway, looking north toward the Friedman home. Friedman's house was on the right-hand side of the street, just around the bend from the last large building shown in the picture.

During a financially good year, the Friedmans acquired a Model T Ford. In the early 1900s the development of the automobile was in its infancy. Safety precautions such as seatbelts, airbags, and shatterproof glass were years away from being developed. Once while riding in the car with his father, Milton fell out and landed on the ground. He was scared, but only suffered a skinned knee. Another time, though, Milton was not as lucky. When one thin wheel of the car struck a rock, Milton's head hit the windshield, and he cut his upper lip. The cut required stitches and left him with a scar and a slightly crooked grin his entire life.

Milton's home life was routine: the parents worked; the children went to school. The girls helped their mother in the store. Rahway had a small Jewish community, but the family did not regularly attend synagogue or observe

Jewish holidays. They spoke English at home. Sarah and Jeno switched to Hungarian only when they wanted to discuss a topic without their children's knowledge.

Milton started school at age five, the same year that the United States joined World War I (the war had begun in 1914, but the U.S. didn't get involved until 1917). The war ended about a year later in November 1918, and while people celebrated a return to normalcy, governments throughout the world moved toward isolationism and social control. President Woodrow Wilson and the U.S. Congress enacted laws to reduce the number of immigrants entering America and to impose higher tariffs on imports. In Russia, Lenin and the Bolsheviks overthrew the traditional autocratic government, signaling the start of the Russian Revolution and Marxist communism.

A colored postcard shows Washington School in Rahway circa 1917, the year five-year-old Milton Friedman entered the grammar school.

It was the Roaring Twenties in America, and while hemlines were rising on skirts and young men and women were spending their earnings dancing and partying at clubs and cheap dance halls, state governments were passing laws making it illegal for the partiers to consume alcoholic drinks. Milton was eight when the Eighteenth Amendment was added to the United States Constitution in 1920 to prevent the manufacture, transport, sale, and consumption of beverages with an alcohol content of 0.5 percent or higher. Many thought that Prohibition would be good for the economy by increasing the productivity of workers and reducing the social burdens of alcoholism. The Eighteenth Amendment, and the Volstead Act passed by the United States Congress to enforce prohibition, had an unintended result, however. It encouraged the illegal production and consumption of alcoholic beverages. The Volstead Act, or Prohibition Act, became one of the most unpopular policies in the history of the United States, and the Eighteenth Amendment was repealed in 1933.

Life in Rahway did not differ much from the pre- and post-war years, however. With Jeno in New York much of the time, Milton grew closer to his mother, who had ambitions for her son in both academics and music. Milton soon discovered that he had no singing talent—his music teacher at school bluntly told him so. Sarah persuaded her son to take violin lessons. Although he dutifully tried to master the instrument, Milton later described himself as a "musical illiterate." He eventually persuaded his mother that the lessons were a waste of time and money that the family could not afford.

Milton had other talents, though. He was ambitious and a good organizer. Upon learning that the only Boy Scout troop available in the area was for Christians, he successfully organized a Jewish Boy Scout troop. He excelled academically, especially in math. In the middle of his sixth grade school year, Milton was promoted early to grade seven.

Milton showed signs of self-discipline at an early age, and he was not afraid to devote a great deal of time and energy to causes. Before the age of twelve, he decided to practice Orthodox Judaism, which, among other traditional practices that his family did not participate in, required that he eat only kosher foods. By age twelve, Milton's religious practices had swung to the opposite end of the continuum; he decided to become agnostic (the doctrine that it's impossible to be certain about the existence of God or any universal ultimate).

This colored postcard shows Rahway High School as it appeared in the late 1920s.

Scarlet and Black

Volume III.   Rahway High School, Rahway, N. J.   Number 2

Published in the Interest of the Pupils of Rahway High School

For Advertising Rates, Address Business Manager   MAY ISSUE 1928

SCARLET AND BLACK EDITORIAL STAFF

Editor-in-Chief	Milton Friedman '28	Alumni Editor	Marie Wilkes '28
Associate	William LaMorte '29	Associate	Amelia Dura '31
Literary Editor	Henrietta Bergen '29	Humor Editor	Robert Shotwell '29
Associate	Harriet Overton '30	Associate	John Jost '31
News Editor	Adam Rankine '28	Art Editor	Evelyn Bracher '30
Associate	Norman Dempster '30	Associate	Frank Applegate '31
Sports Editor	Theodore Landenberger '28	Business Manager	Raymond Reisner '28
Associate	Charles Mauren '29	Associate	
Exchange Editor	Kramer Morrison '29	Faculty Advisor	
Associate	Lester Miller '30	Typists	Mr. Cla

HOME ROOM REPRESENTATIVES

B—1	Ruth Dean '31	C—3	Ch
B—2	Maskell Ewing '30	C—4	
B—3	George Bartell '30	C—5	
B—5	George Lang '30	C—6	
C—1	Russell Post '29	C—7	
C—2	Dorothy Jacobs '29	D—2	

FROM THE OFFIC

EUGENE G. SMEATHERS, *Principal*

Rivalry or competition like so many other things may
not necessarily evil. Some of us are accustomed to think
because of the poor sportsmanship of some people who en

There is a great deal of rivalry in our school of the fine
to note. In Athletics our candidates have shown commendable spirit in competition with rival schools. Custom has decreed that there should be rivalry be-

SCARLET
AND
BLACK

G. O. Number of 1928

RAHWAY HIGH SCHOOL
Rahway, N. J.

Milton Friedman is listed as editor-in-chief in this page from Rahway High School's May 1928 literary magazine, *Scarlet and Black*.

Jeno and Sarah wished for their son, agnostic or not, to
go through the Jewish coming-of-age ceremony, the bar
mitzvah, and Milton obliged their request. He dutifully
attended Hebrew school to study some biblical history
and to learn enough Hebrew to be able to recite the
prayers and responses at the ceremony. At the traditional age of thirteen, he had his bar mitzvah.

Between 1924 and 1928 Milton attended Rahway High School. Smart, talkative and funny, he was one of the youngest and shortest students. If difficult to spot in a crowd, he usually could be heard, because his voice was loud. He joined the baseball team as an assistant manager, and the chess club. Although socialism was creeping across countries in Eastern Europe, times were generally good in America. Employment rates were high, and radio stations were in the infant stages of broadcasting.

Things were not so good for the Friedman family, however. Jeno was not well. For years he had suffered from heart problems. The nitroglycerin pills he took regularly were his only relief for the pains in his chest resulting from inadequate blood flow to his heart. In 1927, as Milton prepared to begin his senior year, Jeno died at age forty-nine.

Milton continued to excel as a student. He developed his oratorical talents and became a skilled debater; he competed in a National Oratorical Contest on the U.S. Constitution sponsored by the *New York Times* and won a bronze medal. Unable to afford to buy books, he spent hours reading and studying in the Rahway public library. His teachers advised him to apply for college. Because of his mother's hard work and frugality, the Friedman family never lacked necessities, such as food and clothing. But Sarah had no extra money for college.

Milton heard about Rutgers, the state university of New Jersey, from two teachers at Rahway High School who were Rutgers graduates. He learned that the state of New Jersey offered tuition scholarships for students who could demonstrate financial need and pass the entrance exam. Milton passed, and received a scholarship to Rutgers in New Brunswick, New Jersey. Milton had the choice of living at home and commuting by train to Rutgers, or moving and living in a dorm. He decided to experience college life at its fullest and moved into Winants Hall dormitory for boys in fall 1928 (the dorm would later become the Rutgers Economics Department).

Living in the dorm meant that sixteen-year-old, five feet three inches tall Milton had to find a job to pay for additional expenses, including his clothing. The economy was booming, and he had no difficulty finding a part-time job as a sales clerk in the men's department at a department store. He worked a twelve-hour day every Saturday and earned thirty-three cents an hour. He took a second job waiting tables during the lunch hour at a small restaurant across the street from Winants Hall. The lunch job caused him to get his only C at Rutgers. His class on European history met at 1:30 PM in a building on the far side of the campus, and Milton was frequently late. The instructor lowered Milton's final grade, not because of poor test scores but because of tardiness. He tried protesting and explaining the situation, but the professor responded that he "was in college not to wait on tables but to learn."

During the summer Milton returned to Rahway and lived at home. He arranged with the principal of Rahway High School to tutor students who had failed courses and needed to take make-up exams. His tutoring sessions included subjects such as mathematics, English, and Latin, and each student paid him fifty cents an hour. He would continue his tutoring job every summer until he graduated from Rutgers. In addition to tutoring, Milton augmented his income with a second job selling fireworks. Portable fireworks stands appeared around town a few weeks before the Fourth of July holiday, and the owner of a stand was often looking for part-time workers. Milton, who had sold fireworks in high school, was known as a reliable worker. He earned about $450 for five weeks of summer work.

When Milton returned to Rutgers in fall 1929, America had begun sliding into the worst depression in history—a catastrophic event that would cause a ripple effect throughout the world. Unemployment in America was increasing because consumers had reduced their spending. It was a vicious cycle, because as unemployment went up, consumer spending declined even more. People had to eat, however, and Milton's mother was

"Variety is the spice of life—and in four years Milt has dabbled in almost every activity, campus and otherwise," noted the editor of Rutgers University's 1932 yearbook. The editor goes on to say of Friedman, whose picture is on the left of this yearbook page, "Argumentation and golf are his favorite by-products. He'll talk you to a frazzle, and enjoy it— what's worse still is that he's usually right."

MILTON FRIEDMAN

Rahway   Liberal Arts

PHI BETA KAPPA

Variety is the spice of life—and in four years Milt has dabbled in almost every activity, campus and otherwise. He manages to crowd three days of life into one, and still maintain a hot pose. He's always ready to do something, regardless of time, place or event. Argumentation and golf are his favorite by-products. He'll talk you to a frazzle, and enjoy it—what's worse still is that he's usually right. He's only taken up golf recently, that is, since Bobby Jones retired; but he'll break a hundred any round now. So good luck, Milt.

Honor School (1, 2, 3, 4); Targum (1, 2), Associate Editor (3), Assistant Editor (4); Mathematics Club (1, 2, 3), Secretary-Treasurer (4); Debating (1, 2); Tennis Manager (1); Neutral Council (4); French Club; German Club.

able to hold onto the dry goods store. His sister Helen had a job as a Western Union telegraph operator. Tillie and Ruth worked at various clerical jobs and at the family's store. At Rutgers, Milton sought ways to earn more money. A friend from Rahway, Harold Harris, joined Milton at Rutgers and was enlisted to help. The two young men became entrepreneurs.

Because freshmen at Rutgers had to wear green ties, Milton and Harold decided to start a small business selling green ties directly to freshmen living in the dorm. Speculating that the freshmen would be willing to pay for the convenience, they presented their plan to the dean of students and received written permission to peddle ties during Freshman Week. The written permission was broad enough that they could expand their peddling to other goods in the future. They purchased their ties from Harold's father, who owned a department store in Rahway. The venture proved very profitable.

When Milton was a junior and Harold a sophomore, the two decided to expand their business and peddle books. They contacted a local book company that agreed to sell textbooks for one day at the beginning of a term. In exchange, Milton and Harold received a 5 percent commission on the profits in exchange for handling the logistical arrangements and advertising. Milton and Harold asked for the right to buy back from the company books at 45 percent of the list price. Again, the company agreed to their terms. They took the initiative to interview professors to ascertain which textbooks would be reused in a subsequent term, then they purchased copies of the textbooks bought by the book company. The plan was to make a profit by selling these textbooks to students during the terms they were needed, at a higher price than what they paid but for lower than what a new book from the company would have cost. When the book company learned about Milton and Harold's plan to sell the discounted books, it protested to the dean of students. But Milton and Harold had the dean's written permission, and he sided with them. Milton and Harold were relieved. The two had borrowed money from Harold's father to finance the purchase of the books. If they had been forbidden to sell the books, they would have lost money. Milton could not afford to make costly financial mistakes. Fortunately, the enterprises were a positive experience and a financial success.

While the free market was good to Milton in the United States, it was perishing in countries such as Germany and Russia. Under Marxist communism, 900 million people—the entire country of Russia and the nearby countries it took over, such as the Ukraine—were experiencing tremendous political, economic, and cultural changes. These countries became known as the Union of Soviet Socialist Republics (USSR). When Lenin died in 1924, Joseph Stalin assumed control of the government. In the name of communism—supposedly for the welfare of all—Stalin began collectivizing agriculture in 1930. Russian farmers watched helplessly as the government confiscated their lands. Anyone who resisted might be exiled to Siberia, or worse. Millions of people were executed or starved to death as food production declined.

In 1930, Milton was much more focused on mathematics and earning a degree than international politics. Once he graduated, Milton planned to get a job in insurance as an actuary, and he began taking some of the

Phi Beta Kappa
ALPHA CHAPTER OF NEW JERSEY
Established 1869

Rev. Milton J. Hoffman...President
Prof. Edmund W. Billetdoux...Vice-President
Prof. George H. Brown...Treasurer
Prof. Edward F. Johnson...Corresponding Secretary
Ernest E. McMahon...Recording Secretary

HONORARY MEMBERS

Dr. Phillip M. Brett   Dr. Millard L. Lowery
Dr. Robert C. Clothier   Prof. Julien Moreno-Lacalle
Dean Parker H. Daggett   Dr. Clarence E. Partch

CLASS OF 1932

Nathan Adelman   Grom M. Hayes
Simon A. Bahr   Robert R. Hendricks
Morris Bailkin   Sidney M. Hodas
John F. Borchers   Louis T. Kardos
Morris L. Cohen   Charles E. Key
Lewis F. Cole   Samuel R. Kirschner
Fred J. Cook   Frederick J. Knauer
Lee W. Courter   Aaron Kotler
Edward F. Drake   Jack Levin
Joseph P. Farkas   Philip Rector
Frederic P. Fischer   Benjamin Shmurak
Milton R. Friedman   Leo H. Schwartz
William H. Glover   Edgar D. Van Wagoner
Harry Von Bulow

This page from the 1932 Rutgers University yearbook shows Milton Friedman (front row, far right) with other Phi Beta Kappa students at the university.

actuarial examinations—passing some and failing some. He became a copy editor for the school newspaper, *Targum*. Also, he completed two years of Reserve Officers Training Corps (ROTC). His coursework consisted of French, German, American government, English, public speaking, chemistry, and economics. In his economics courses, Milton met two men who would have a significant impact on his career: Arthur F. Burns and Homer Jones.

Arthur Burns, eight years older than Milton, was teaching economics at Rutgers while finishing his doctoral studies at Columbia University in New York. At Rutgers he taught Milton only one course—business cycles, and yet Burns became somewhat of a surrogate father. Like Milton's parents, Burns, an Austrian, had immigrated to the United States. Upon his arrival at age seventeen he spoke no English, but he had worked hard and prospered. Now he was teaching at a major university and completing his doctorate.

Homer Jones, an Iowa farm boy, had graduated from the University of Iowa, where he was a protégé of economist Frank H. Knight. When Knight moved and became a professor at the University of Chicago, Jones followed as a graduate student. Knight was an influential and popular professor who believed in capitalism and the free market, and Jones eagerly followed his example. He was twenty-four when he taught Milton at Rutgers. The instructor taught principles of insurance and statistical methods courses, and he passed on to his students Knight's theories and ideas on individual freedom.

Milton Friedman abandoned his actuarial career goals. He graduated Phi Beta Kappa in 1932 with a degree in economics. Encouraged by his professors, he applied for tuition scholarships at several universities to pursue a graduate degree. Brown University offered him a scholarship to study applied mathematics, while the University of Chicago, Jones's alma mater, offered him a scholarship to study economics. Given the economic crisis of the Great Depression, being an economist seemed much more important to the idealistic young Friedman than applied mathematics. In referencing the famous Robert Frost poem, "The Road Not Taken," Friedman said years later, "I cannot say I took the less traveled one, but the one I took determined the whole course of my life."

2 Capitalism at Risk

Milton Friedman, who had no car, rode with a couple of college friends to Chicago. While a student at Rutgers, Friedman had been frugal with his hard-earned money. Despite the most devastating depression in United States history, he had managed to save two hundred dollars. Even so, he knew the money would not last long. Upon arriving in Chicago in fall 1932, twenty-year-old Friedman set out to find a cheap place to live and a job.

Once again resourcefulness helped. Friedman met an elderly widow who owned a small restaurant near the University of Chicago campus. Above the restaurant were some rooms she rented. In exchange for working at the restaurant part-time, especially on crowded football game days, Friedman got a room and one meal a day. Next he found a part-time job working as a salesman at a shoe store on Saturdays. Rather than earning an hourly or daily wage, he received a commission on the number of shoes sold. Long hours and hard work did not deter Friedman; unfortunately, the department's seniority system did. The clerk who had worked at the store the longest had first right to assist a customer, followed by the second-longest-working employee, and so on. Being the new hire, Friedman had to wait until every clerk in the shoe department was assisting a customer before he could get a turn. He worked twelve hours and earned seventy-five cents his first day on the job. His training as an economist had taught him the value of his time and effort—or his opportunity cost. He quit and relied on his savings and loans from his family (primarily sister Helen who worked as a telegraph operator) to support himself that first year of graduate school.

The University of Chicago was founded in 1892. John D. Rockefeller had donated an astounding $35 million—an amount equal to about $1 billion in 2008— to help get the university started. Compared to universities in the East, some of which had been founded in the 1600s, the University of Chicago was relatively new when Friedman matriculated in 1932. Yet the institution already had a reputation for having one of the best departments of economics in the country because of its distinguished faculty and bright students, many of whom were foreigners. Debating was a common practice among faculty and students, and Friedman relished debating. He recalled that "Controversies among faculty members, mostly on an intellectual basis, helped to make the department an exciting place to study, preserved an atmosphere of a search for truth, and developed the tradition that what mattered in intellectual discourse was only the cogency of an argument, not the diplomacy with which it was stated, or the seniority or professional standing of the person who stated it." The distinguished professors in the department included

Unemployed men wait in line outside a Chicago soup kitchen, February 1931. At the depths of the Great Depression—a worldwide economic downturn that began during the late 1920s—one in four American workers was jobless.

Frank Knight—Homer Jones's (Friedman's mentor at Rutgers) former teacher and mentor.

Born in 1885, Frank Knight was bald, with a little gray mustache and a round, pink face and glasses. In his history of economic thought course, Knight imbued in his students the importance of skepticism in the search for reason and truth. Also, he discussed the ideas of individualism and liberty, including the importance of a free-market system.

A second distinguished faculty member was Jacob Viner. A stern master with a reputation for failing a third of the class, Viner made economic theory colorful and exciting. Quick and articulate, Viner demanded that his students come to class prepared, and he frequently called upon them to answer questions. If a student repeatedly failed to answer correctly, it was not uncommon for Viner to tell him or her to leave. Friedman appreciated Viner's class, first for expanding his knowledge and understanding of economics and second for introducing him to a most unusual person—a female student enrolled in the doctorate program. Viner seated his students in alphabetical order, and in his Econ 301 Price and Distribution course, Friedman was seated next to Rose Director.

Rose Director was most likely born in December 1911 in Charterisk, Russia, now part of the Ukraine. At the age of two she and her mother immigrated to Portland, Oregon, where they were reunited with Rose's

Frank Knight (1885–1972) presided over the University of Chicago's Department of Economics from the late 1920s to the early 1940s. Knight held strong beliefs about risk, free markets, and the capitalist system. These led him to criticize the theories or methods of several of the leading economists of his day, including John Maynard Keynes and A. C. Pigou.

father and siblings: two older sisters and two older brothers. Brother Aaron, nine years older than Rose, was responsible for bringing his sister to the University of Chicago. In 1932, he was teaching as a junior member of the economics faculty at the University of Chicago and completing his graduate studies in economics. Aaron was both mentor and brother to Rose; also, he provided financial support. Because she did not want to disappoint him, Rose worked hard to make good grades and a good impression. She had few close friends, and was one of the few female graduate students at any university in the 1930s.

Rose and Friedman discovered that they shared much in common. Like Friedman, Rose had excelled academically, and graduated early from high school at the age of sixteen. Shy and pretty, she was five feet two inches tall, about one inch shorter than him. They also were very much alike when it came to important philosophical views, especially about politics and economics, and both had been raised Jewish. Studying economics in the midst of a severe depression, the two students were swept into the debate of how much government involvement is necessary to fix the economy.

Years later the political philosopher Lanny Ebenstein would write that during the 1930s, when Rose and Friedman were studying at the University of Chicago, many economists argued effectively that the Great Depression had been "caused by excesses in the capitalist system: Unscrupulous speculators buying stocks on margin forced prices up in an orgy of greed that inevitably ended in the great stock market crash of

October 1929." (Buying on margin means financing much of the purchase with borrowed money.)

Some prominent economists thought the Great Depression was a sign that capitalism was fundamentally flawed, and many intellectuals and politicians agreed. Some began to believe that Karl Marx, who had predicted the collapse of capitalism, was right and Adam Smith, who had established economics as a separate academic subject by arguing market economies worked the best, was wrong. Socialism and collectivism were better for society than capitalism and individualism, they argued. Such debates had endured for years, but the Great Depression gave the anti-capitalists the catalyst they needed. Eastern Europe, parts of Asia, even areas of South America, already had become socialist. Germany appeared to be at risk. Socialist organizations were proliferating in America and western Europe as well.

In 1932, with the United States economy still in a severe depression, economists on the side of less government, such as Frank Knight, were a minority and generally disregarded. Economists on the side of more government, such as John Maynard Keynes, were considered saviors. Keynes, a prominent British economist, had advocated more government intervention—including more government spending—in the 1920s to reduce high unemployment in England, though he was not a socialist. As a result of the Great Depression, his ideas gained importance.

Keynes believed that to fix the depressed economies in America and Great Britain and prevent another devas-

The Great Depression led growing numbers of people to subscribe to the views of the German philosopher Karl Marx (1818–1883), who believed that socialist societies would replace capitalist ones. Socialism is an economic and political system in which the state not only owns factories and raw materials but also oversees the production and distribution of goods.

tating depression, governments must intervene and direct the economy rather than rely on market forces to restore full employment and economic prosperity. He argued that increasing government spending and lowering taxes would restore full employment. That this practice led to large government budget deficits was considered of little importance by Keynes and his disciples. Adam Smith had argued one hundred and fifty-six years earlier in his famous book, *The Wealth of Nations*, for thriftiness among individuals and governments. But Keynes now advocated a different doctrine from that of Smith's. According to the British economist and colleague of Keynes, Sir Roy Harrod, Keynes argued that "On the contrary, in times of depression and unemployment it was desirable to encourage spending and lavishness."

Before the Great Depression, prominent economists at Harvard, such as Alvin Hanson, accepted Keynes's theory, and by the end of the Depression Keynesianism had become a major movement in economics. Throughout the 1930s and up until his death in 1946, Keynes traveled across the Atlantic Ocean many times, advising government officials in America on economic policies.

Friedman and Rose were introduced to Keynes's theories at Chicago. Friedman took a course on monetary theory with Professor Mints, in which one of the assigned readings was Keynes's book *A Treatise on Money*. Friedman discovered that he and Keynes had something in common besides economics—both were trained and skilled mathematicians. When the United States government began a policy of deficit spending based on Keynesian economics, Friedman approved.

During Friedman's first year at Chicago, Franklin Roosevelt was elected president on his New Deal platform to save America. The New Deal began a swift proliferation of government policies and programs to improve the economy. Almost immediately, Congress began increasing regulation of economic activity, including regulating the sale of securities on the stock exchange. New governmental agencies were created, such as the Federal Deposit Insurance Corporation (FDIC) to regulate savings-bank deposits, and the Civilian Conservation Corps (CCC), a program designed to put young men between eighteen and twenty-five years old to work on various public works projects, including planting trees to combat soil erosion and creating bird sanctuaries. Projects by the Public Works Administration (PWA) included building two aircraft carriers for the Navy, Grand Coulee Dam in the Pacific Northwest, and a new sewer system in Chicago.

Yet the Depression continued. The recovery plan called for the United States government to spend $300 million a month. Keynes advised the government to spend more, at least $400 million a month. The proliferation of new government agencies and programs required hiring thousands of personnel who began moving to Washington, D.C.

The 1933 Chicago World's Fair, A Century of Progress, began the same year that Adolf Hitler became chancellor of Germany and built the first Nazi concentration camp. Friedman, Rose, and a graduate student from Sweden, Sune Carlson, went to the fair. Upon returning to the campus later that night, Carlson left Friedman and Rose sitting on a bench discussing the future. Friedman had been offered a lucrative fellowship at Columbia University in New York that would pay him to pursue graduate studies for his doctorate. The annual stipend was $1,500 and he needed the money. Both he and Carlson had decided to move to New York City to attend Columbia University in the fall. Before parting that evening, Friedman attempted a goodnight kiss. Rose later recalled that she "refused to cooperate." With Friedman living in New York and her in Chicago, the prospect of their friendship turning to romance did not look good.

Friedman graduated with a master's degree in economics from the University of Chicago. He then moved

A worker places a National Recovery Administration (NRA) poster in the window of a restaurant. Established in 1933, the NRA created voluntary codes for business owners on issues such as minimum pay, maximum work hours, and unionization. It was part of President Franklin D. Roosevelt's New Deal, an array of government programs intended to help pull the U.S. economy out of the Great Depression.

to New York City for the fall 1933 term. Once he had received his stipend money from Columbia, he paid back his debt of $300 to Helen and other family members. He paid $300 for tuition, leaving $900 to cover his dormitory room, meals, and other expenses for the rest of the year.

Columbia University was founded in 1754 and is the fifth-oldest institute of higher education in the United States. In the economics department at Columbia in the 1930s, emphasis was placed on learning methods to measure economic activity, and the twenty-one-year-old Friedman found that his mathematical and statistical skills served him well. He also enjoyed living in New York City. The city's skyline was undergoing a dramatic change. The Empire State Building, the world's tallest building, had opened in May 1931. He took advantage of the city's entertainment by paying five cents to ride the subway from his dorm to Times Square to buy discounted theater tickets. He also enjoyed going to the Savoy Ballroom in Harlem. Still, his interest in Chicago had not disappeared. He had good friends in Chicago, including Rose.

Rose spent the summer of 1934 with her parents in Portland and returned to Chicago in the fall to continue her graduate studies. Her brother Aaron had lost his job and was moving to Washington, D.C., to work in the Treasury Department. He had not received tenure, primarily because he had sided with Frank Knight in a controversy that divided the economics faculty. Fortunately for Rose, Frank Knight offered her a research assistantship position that would allow her to be financially independent from Aaron and yet continue her graduate studies. Friedman, too, was offered a research assistantship position at the University of Chicago. He agreed and became a research assistant for the economist Professor Henry Schultz. In the fall, Friedman moved back to Chicago.

Upon his return to Chicago, Friedman met two students who would become close friends throughout his lifetime—George Stigler and Allen Wallis. Stigler was dating Margaret Mack and Wallis was dating Anne Armstrong. Along with Rose, they all frequently socialized together. Rose recalled later that Anne and

Margaret were very accommodating, because the topic of discussion was usually "economics, economics, economics."

Friedman's assistantship paid $1,600 for the year. Also, his tuition fees were waived. During the year he took courses and passed examinations for the Ph.D. degree in economics. He benefited professionally from assisting Professor Schultz and took pleasure in the work assignments. His primary assignment was to review a manuscript that Professor Schultz had written on statistical demand curves, suggest changes, and draft revisions for Schultz to consider. Schultz entrusted Friedman to check all the facts for accuracy. The book was titled *The Theory and Measurement of Demand*.

Friedman also wrote an article for publication, which criticized the work of a well-known British economist, Professor A. C. Pigou, a distinguished don at Cambridge University. Friedman disagreed with Professor Pigou's method of using budgetary data to measure elasticities of demand (how sensitive the amount of a good demanded is to its price) and decided to go public in explaining why Pigou was wrong. Friedman brazenly submitted his article to the editor of the *Economic Journal*, none other than the famous Cambridge Professor John Maynard Keynes. Keynes rejected the article, acknowledging in his letter to Friedman that he had discussed the article with Pigou.

Undeterred, Friedman submitted the article to Professor F. W. Taussig, editor of the *Quarterly Journal of Economics* at Harvard University. Professor Taussig accepted the article, and it was published in the

November 1935 issue. Professor Pigou sent a letter to Taussig objecting to the publication of Friedman's critical article. Fortunately, Friedman had apprised Taussig in advance that the article was previously submitted to Keynes and rejected. Professor Taussig allowed academic freedom to persevere. Pigou wrote a reply to Friedman's article; it and Friedman's rejoinder were both published in the May 1936 issue of the journal. Both Pigou and Friedman were ultimately correct. Pigou's argument was correct when the good demanded took only a small amount of the consumer's budget. Friedman was correct in

Milton and Rose Friedman in the 1930s. The two met as graduate students at the University of Chicago.

pointing this out and generalizing the analysis to cover all goods, no matter how much is spent on them.

Friedman enjoyed his year in Chicago. He spent evenings in stimulating intellectual conversations on economics and world events with his close friends Rose, Stigler, and Wallis. Regarding world events there was much to discuss, including the new chancellor of Germany, Adolf Hitler, and the spread of communism. Friedman and Rose were now romantically involved and his academic studies were going well. Yet Friedman decided to take a hiatus from the doctoral program and seek work that offered more money and job stability. He discovered that there were few teaching jobs available at colleges and universities, and, being Jewish, he believed he would have little chance of getting a position because of anti-Semitism. In 1935, the Roosevelt administration's New Deal was in its third year and gaining momentum. New jobs were being created regularly, and economists and statisticians were in high demand.

Allen Wallis had already left Chicago and moved to Washington, D.C., to work at the National Resources Committee (NRC). On August 19, 1935, Friedman joined Wallis at NRC. Friedman's reasons for moving to Washington were not so much that he saw himself as a political crusader. Rather, he moved because of the practical fact that it was time to make more money and the best chance of finding a well-paying job for an economist was in Washington, D.C. Friedman found a room to rent from Lois and Ellsworth Clark. His annual salary that first year was $2,600.

3

Petty Politics

t the National Resources Committee (NRC),
Friedman joined a team created to undertake the
first comprehensive national study of consumer
income and purchases. The political philosopher Lanny
Ebenstein later wrote that this effort was the beginning
of years of study that Friedman would devote to "the
consumption function—the relationship between consumption and income." Friedman's role on the team
was that of a technician, utilizing his statistical and
mathematical abilities.

In the 1930s, computers and easy-to-use hand cal-
culators were not available. The process of analyzing
the massive amounts of data collected was limited and
slow, and it took hours, even days, to make the calcula-
tions that can now be done in seconds. Consequently,
research projects were exorbitantly expensive.
Friedman appreciated the challenge of his assignment,
and regarded his experience at NRC as excellent training for furthering his career.

Friedman and Rose missed seeing one another, however. She considered getting a job in Washington, D.C.,
where she could work and write her dissertation on

weekends. They constantly wrote letters to one another. He visited Chicago one weekend, and the two discussed the possibility of her moving to Washington to work. But Rose was not a U.S. citizen. Earlier in her life she had started the application process but never finished because she had been able to obtain jobs without the citizenship papers. The jobs she qualified for in Washington were different; they required citizenship. Friends—and friends of friends—joined together to expedite Rose's application for citizenship. Before long everything was arranged, and she was offered a job at the Division of Research and Statistics of the Federal Deposit Insurance Corporation.

Both in their twenties, Friedman and Rose thrived in D.C. They later recalled, "We had the feeling—or illusion—that we were in at the birth of a new order that

Cherry trees bloom along the Potomac River, with the Washington Monument in the background. Milton Friedman moved to Washington, D.C., in 1935 to take a position with the National Resources Committee.

would lead to major changes in society." Even though the two enjoyed living in Washington, in 1937 an opportunity arose to advance Friedman's career.

He moved to New York on September 20 to work as an assistant to Simon Kuznets at the National Bureau of Economic Research (NBER). When Friedman moved out of the room he rented, Rose moved in. She would not remain in Washington for more than a year, as their future plans called for her to follow him to New York.

Friedman's primary assignment at NBER was to revise and complete Kuznets's early draft of a manuscript on the incomes of independent professional practitioners. First, though, he would have to complete the statistical analysis of the data Kuznets had gathered. The manuscript, *Incomes from Independent Professional Practice*, would take eight years to complete. While the subsequent publication of the book would become an important step in completing the dissertation requirements for Friedman's Ph.D., it also would be a contributing factor in its delay.

Friedman, always looking for ways to increase his earnings, began teaching part-time at Columbia University. He had also retained a role at NRC as a consultant, which allowed him to travel to Washington regularly (his expenses paid) to visit Rose and further augment his salary. Because airplane travel between New York and Washington was expensive, he traveled by train, and the trip took six hours or more one-way. Friedman and Rose decided they would marry when she moved to New York. For ten long months he commuted to Washington whenever possible. The happily engaged couple exchanged letters weekly, gladly paying three cents for a postal stamp.

The marriage ceremony was scheduled for June 25, 1938, in New York City. Rose's parents and siblings could not make the long trip across country and attend the wedding, and she traveled to Portland to visit them beforehand. She returned to New York three days before the ceremony. In honor of their parents' wishes, the ceremony was held at a Jewish seminary. Aaron Director was in England teaching at the London School of Economics and could not attend. Those in attendance at the traditional Orthodox Jewish ceremony included Friedman's mother, sisters, a brother-in-law, a few New York friends and their former landlords in Washington, D.C., Lois and Ellsworth Clark.

Friedman had purchased an automobile, and the morning after the wedding he and Rose, along with all of their personal possessions, drove to North Lovell, Maine, for the honeymoon. Their rented stone cottage was in the woods with a view of Lake Kezar. The house had no electricity, and they cooked their food on the wood-burning stove. Afternoons were spent canoeing, hiking, or swimming—after Friedman taught Rose how to swim. At night they lit kerosene lamps and worked on their doctoral dissertations. The couple shared the chores, and typed each other's manuscripts. Rose, the better cook, prepared the meals, and Friedman chopped wood for the stove. Rose said years later, "It was never a question of woman's work or man's work. It was only a question of who had the comparative advantage, including the time for the job at hand."

Upon their return to New York City weeks later, the couple rented an apartment a few subway stops from Friedman's office. It did not take them long to unpack. The two had agreed to buy the necessary furnishings with cash and not credit; therefore, furnishing the apartment did not happen quickly. Friedman, using carpentry skills learned back in high school, spent his spare time building bookcases.

Another significant event for Friedman in 1938 was the publication of Professor Henry Schultz's book, *The Theory and Measurement of Demand*, which Friedman had helped the Chicago professor write back in 1934. Unfortunately, the professor did not live long after his book was published. The forty-five-year-old Schultz, who had recently learned to drive, took his wife and children in their newly purchased automobile to California for a vacation. Two days after the Thanksgiving holiday they were driving along the scenic but narrow and winding U.S. Route 1, when for some unknown reason the car veered, plunging down a steep cliff. Schultz and his family died.

Rose found a job working on a cooperative project between the National Bureau of Economic Research, the Federal Deposit Insurance Corporation, and the Federal Reserve Bankers Association. She and Friedman socialized regularly with friends, and the animated dinner party conversations usually included the same two topics: economics and the seemingly inevitable war in Europe.

On September 3, 1939, England and France declared war on Germany after Hitler's army invaded

Poland. World War II had begun. Remembering the human casualties and financial devastation caused by the First World War, initially the United States maintained a policy of neutrality.

Friedman received an offer of a one-year visiting professor appointment to teach at the University of Wisconsin in Madison for the 1940–1941 school year, which he accepted. His salary was $4,000 for teaching two statistics courses in the economics department and assisting Harold Groves, a professor of public finance, with a research project—a study of Wisconsin incomes. Friedman and Rose resigned from their jobs and spent several weeks that summer exploring different parts of the United States and visiting Rose's family and friends in Oregon. Besides knowing Rose's brother Aaron at the University of Chicago, Friedman had met her mother when she visited them in New York. The visit to Portland was his first meeting with his father-in-law and Rose's other siblings, however.

One memorable part of the trip was a Grand Canyon adventure. They decided to ride burros down into the canyon rather than hike, and that night, both stood to eat their dinner because of the pain caused by riding in the uncomfortable saddles. During the long trip they ventured south and north to visit parts of Mexico and Canada. In Canada they ran into trouble. Rounding a curve after a heavy rainstorm, they hit a wet spot on the road, and their Kaiser convertible skidded and turned over. Fortunately, the top was up because of the storm, and they managed to crawl out from under the car. Automobiles did not come equipped with seat belts in

Bascom Hall on the campus of the University of Wisconsin at Madison, where Milton Friedman taught in 1940–1941.

those days, but unlike Professor Schultz and his family, both Friedman and Rose were unhurt. The badly damaged car was towed to a nearby town where they waited for it to be repaired. Friedman and Rose said years later that they thought themselves "born under a lucky star."

Soon after arriving at the University of Wisconsin for the start of the fall term, Friedman found himself entangled in departmental politics. Rose had witnessed such a situation before, at the University of Chicago when departmental politics had caused Aaron to lose his job. Initially, Professor Harold Groves had intended to offer Friedman a full-time permanent teaching position, but he could not obtain a majority of the faculty votes. Groves sought to strengthen the statistics and economic theory courses to advance the economic department's rankings among universities, and he believed that hiring Milton Friedman would help. But several professors opposed Grove's plan, especially those professors currently teaching statistics and economic theory courses who thought their positions were being threatened. When Grove's attempt to grant Friedman a full-time position was rejected, a compromise was arranged offering Friedman a one-year appointment instead. Still, Groves hoped to gather enough votes within the next twelve months to offer Friedman a permanent position.

Because of the political division in the department, Friedman and Rose had little social contact with the other professors and their families. They made friends with many of the students, though. Rose wrote years later that their "home was always open to students, and the more mature among them took advantage of the opportunity." Rose did not work. She took pottery courses, and soon she became pregnant. She suffered from morning nausea and generally did not feel well, which resulted in more than one brief stay at a hospital. Friedman spent the year caring for Rose and pondering his future at Wisconsin.

For the next several months, Groves continued lobbying and negotiating, trying to get the professors who opposed the offer of a permanent position for Friedman to change their votes. When it was clear that Groves would not get the votes he needed, he and the Dean of the College of Letters and Science circumvented the opposing faculty members by going directly to the university's president. The president agreed with Groves and the dean, and Friedman was offered a permanent position at Wisconsin. He accepted the offer.

Unfortunately, the petty university politics did not end. The opposition staged a protest and contacted the local media. Although he had not caused the rivalry between the two factions in the economics department, he was definitely caught in the middle. As Friedman later recalled, he had become "a pawn in an internal departmental controversy." Friedman and Rose decided against staying at Wisconsin, and he wrote to the president withdrawing his name as a candidate.

At the end of the one-year faculty appointment, Friedman drove back to New York while Rose traveled by train because of her pregnancy. Once in New York they continued on in the car to Norwich, Vermont (which became a regular summer home for them), to relax and make plans for the future. Throughout the summer Friedman worked on a project—the use of taxes to prevent inflation—for the Treasury Department. Other friends from Columbia and NBER were summering near-by. Although the pregnancy still was not going well, he and Rose managed to spend some time socializing.

The couple returned to New York City in July to prepare for the baby's arrival. It was a difficult delivery, and the infant boy was stillborn. Rose wrote years later, "As I look back, this blow was more devastating to us than our Wisconsin experience. However, sharing the pain of both of these experiences seemed to bring Milton and me even closer than we already were. In addition, we were no longer children; suddenly we had grown up."

Friedman accepted a job with the Division of Tax Research of the Treasury Department, and he and Rose prepared to return to Washington, D.C. Aaron Director had returned to the United States from his teaching job at the London School of Economics and was living in

Maryland. Friedman and Rose planned on living with Aaron in an old farmhouse he had purchased, even though the house was a long commute from Friedman's office in Washington. Prior to the move, Lois Clark took Rose to see the house. After making the long drive through the rural country on a gray and rainy day and seeing the run-down house, both agreed that the Friedmans would find an apartment in Washington.

Friedman's government job in 1937 had been that of a technician in statistics and economics. He was mostly excluded from any bickering and infighting that tend to go with politics. This job was different. It required that he be more involved in the political process, and with politicians. He had to write testimony, brief legislators, and testify before congressional committees, such as the Senate Finance Committee, to get legislation enacted. Friedman said, "I came to understand firsthand the pull that Washington has for so many intellectuals, the sense of shaping the destiny of a nation, the excitement of the political process—and also experienced the manipulation, dishonesty, and self-seeking that are an intrinsic part of the process."

When the Japanese bombed Pearl Harbor, Hawaii, on December 7, 1941, the United States abandoned its policy of neutrality and entered World War II. Treasury Department officials were responsible for raising money to finance the war. They wanted to avoid the problems encountered during World War I from borrowing money at high interest rates and creating high inflation (the price level increased as much as 20 percent a year during World War I). This time Treasury officials wanted to

The photo—taken from a Japanese warplane on December 7, 1941—shows American battleships moored at Pearl Harbor, Hawaii, at the start of the surprise attack that pulled the United States into World War II.

pay for the war primarily by raising taxes, instead of borrowing and running large federal budget deficits. When Friedman joined the recently expanded Division of Tax Research, strategies were already being developed to revise the tax structure, including personal and corporate income taxes, excise taxes, estate taxes, and gift taxes.

Keynesian theory prevailed at the Treasury Department. Keynes's 1940 book, *How to Pay for the War: A Radical Plan for the Chancellor of the Exchequer*, was a blueprint for legislation that would reduce private spending by increasing taxes. Running large budget deficits was a good idea, according to Keynes, in a depression, but not during a war, when large government spending would be inflationary unless private spending was reduced. Keynes, the editor of the *Economic Journal*, may have rejected Friedman's article in 1934, but Friedman held no grudges. In 1941, he considered himself "thoroughly Keynesian."

Consistent with Keynes's recommendation to increase taxes, Friedman helped get a policy of withholding income taxes passed. Prior to 1942, any individual working in America was responsible for paying his or her own income taxes. Each person paid his or her income tax based on the earnings of the previous year in four installments. In the new withholding system, employers deducted taxes from the paycheck and paid the required tax on behalf of the employee. Having to pay taxes by writing checks to the government was

The British economist John Maynard Keynes (1883–1946) recommended paying for World War II by increasing taxes. During the 1930s and 1940s, Keynes's economic theories—which included increased government spending on public projects in order to reduce the negative effects of the business cycle (depressions and recessions)—were adopted by the governments of many Western nations, including the United States.

Henry Morgenthau (1891–1967) served as secretary of the Treasury during the time Milton Friedman worked for the Division of Tax Research. Personally, Morgenthau disagreed with Keynesian economic theories—he disapproved of government borrowing and believed that public spending would not stimulate the economy. However, during his twelve years as head of the Treasury, Morgenthau supported Roosevelt's New Deal programs.

more painful than having them withheld a little at a time by an employer. Therefore, the policy of withholding taxes made it easier for the federal government to raise and collect taxes during the war.

When Friedman and other Treasury officials rushed to revise the tax structure, there was almost no consideration of the long run. Tax withholding continued after the war and made it easier for the federal government to keep taxes and government spending higher than they would have been otherwise. Friedman would later express regret that he was instrumental in expanding government beyond what he considered desirable.

Friedman and his colleagues in the Division of Tax Research strategized on the best methods for presenting their recommendations and getting them accepted. To increase the chances of getting proposals read, three typewriters were purchased: one with large type, one with regular type, and one with small type. Because Secretary of the Treasury Henry Morgenthau did not regularly wear his glasses and did not care whether a letter was one page or more, letters and proposals sent to him were in large type. The small type was used for President Roosevelt, who restricted letters to one page. Friedman learned to explain complex and technical materials for men and women who were responsible for setting economic policies, but who knew nothing about economics.

Years later, Friedman also noted that working at the Treasury taught him an important lesson: "It is far easier to introduce a government program than to get rid of it."

At the age of thirty, Rose became pregnant again. A healthy baby girl, Janet Friedman, was born on February 26, 1943. Three days later Friedman left for New York City and a new job. He was following the advice he would later pass on to his students: "by all means spend a few years in Washington—but only a few. If you stay more than two or three you will become addicted and will be unable effectively to return to a scholarly career."

4 Professor Friedman

riedman commuted on weekends for two months until Rose and Janet joined him in New York. The Friedmans' old friend Allen Wallis was the director of the Statistical Research Group (SRG), located at Columbia University. Friedman was the associate director, and their good friend George Stigler worked at SRG also. This new organization had been created in 1942 to mobilize scientists to help in the war effort. Economists, physicists, chemists, statisticians, and mathematicians had agreed to work at SRG—many of them taking a leave of absence from their jobs—to improve the effectiveness of the military. Friedman worked directly with various members of the Army, Navy, Air Force, and Marines, and the job was highly confidential. For the first time in their marriage Friedman could not share his work with Rose. Every night he locked up all classified materials and documents before leaving the office, and it was the first, and only, time that he kept a clean desk.

From 1943 through summer 1945, Friedman traveled to military bases to meet with military personnel and conduct studies, such as evaluating the effectiveness of

In 1942, Allen Wallis (1912–1998) invited his good friend Milton Friedman to join the U.S. Office of Scientific Research's Statistical Research Group (SRG). After the war, Wallis went on to become dean of the University of Chicago Graduate School of Business (1956–1962) and serve as president and chancellor of the University of Rochester (1962–1970). He also advised four U.S. presidents: Eisenhower, Nixon, Ford, and Reagan.

anti-aircraft shells, and the vulnerability of bomber planes including the B-29 and B-17. In Alamogordo, New Mexico, he rode in a small plane to experience firsthand what a pilot would do to take evasive action from an enemy. The ride left him queasy and bruised after he hit his head mid-flight.

The year 1945 was eventful both personally and professionally for the Friedmans. Their second child, David Director Friedman, was born on February 12, 1945. Rose's sister Becky traveled across the country to New York to care for the energetic Janet until Rose recovered. The apartment had no washing machine or dishwasher, and the women had to go down to the basement of the building to wash the many loads of dirty diapers. Gas was rationed, so they used public transportation for shopping.

As World War II came to an end, the SRG projects began to wind down. George Stigler, on leave of absence from his academic position at the University of Minnesota, helped Friedman to get a one-year faculty appointment at Minnesota in the economics department. Friedman, Rose, Janet, and David moved to Minnesota in time for the 1945 fall term.

At the University of Minnesota, Friedman taught two courses each semester: statistics and economics. He shared an office with Stigler, and would later recall that the two "lived, breathed, and slept economics." Stigler, slim and about 6'3" tall, towered over his diminutive friend. He had a sharp wit, and set high standards in the classroom. When a student once complained that he did not deserve the F grade he had received, Professor Stigler quickly agreed, saying that unfortunately it was the lowest grade he could give. The Friedmans and the Stiglers (George had married his girlfriend Margaret

George Stigler (1911–1991) was, along with Milton Friedman, one of the most prominent members of the so-called Chicago School of economic thought that emerged during the twentieth century. Stigler would receive a Nobel Prize in Economics in 1982.

Mack) socialized regularly, often making time during their hours of discussing economics and world affairs to play bridge.

Rose had abandoned her plan to complete her Ph.D. degree, but Friedman had not. Ten years had passed since he had successfully completed his doctoral courses and examinations, and he should have had his degree from Columbia by now. But Columbia had one unusual final requirement: a student had to have a dissertation published before it would award the Ph.D.

Friedman's dissertation was the paper he had coauthored with Simon Kuznets for NBER back in 1937— *Income from Independent Professional Practice*. Between 1938 and 1941, Friedman had revised the paper, and it was ready for publication. But publication had been delayed because of disagreement among certain NBER members who did not approve of Kuznets and Friedman's criticism of the American Medical Association (AMA).

In the paper, Kuznets and Friedman argued that physicians made more money (by one-third) than certain other professional groups, such as dentists, because the AMA restricted entrance by reducing the number of students accepted into medical school. Kuznets and Friedman concluded that restricting the supply of physicians available to treat people increased the prices that physicians charged their patients. The coauthors believed that the AMA purposely restricted entrance, not because of standards and concerns for patient safety, but because the AMA wanted physicians to earn higher incomes. The NBER approval committee refused to release the paper for publication without unanimous consensus. Friedman could not receive his Ph.D. until the paper was published. Finally, the director of the bureau, Wesley Clair Mitchell, intervened on Friedman's behalf. The paper was published in 1945, and he acquired the title of Dr. Milton Friedman.

Before completing his one-year contract at the University of Minnesota, Friedman was offered a permanent, tenured associate professor position. He and Rose found their experience at Minnesota intellectually stimulating and socially delightful. He liked teaching. Friedman accepted the tenured position.

The following year George Stigler was a candidate for a professorship at the University of Chicago. If he accepted he would assume Jacob Viner's position, since Viner had taken a job at Princeton. Stigler was approved by the economics department faculty committee, but he still had to obtain final approval from the university's central administration. Stigler met with the university president, who vetoed his appointment. The next candidate considered was Friedman, and after proceeding through the interview process, he received the offer. The opportunity of a professorship at the University of Chicago was too lucrative to pass up, and Friedman accepted. Fortunately, the disappointed Stigler and the jubilant Friedman remained good friends. There was a second significant hire that year at Chicago. Allen Wallis joined the faculty of the University of Chicago Graduate School of Business to teach statistics. Soon, the Wallises and the Friedmans were together again in Illinois.

Rose, three-year-old Janet, one-year-old David, and Friedman moved to Chicago in September 1946. They bought an old three-story brick house with a basement for Friedman's carpentry tools and workshop. The house was a short walk to restaurants and small shops. It had enough space for four people to live comfortably, as well as Friedman's messy desk. Friedman could walk to his office at the university in about seven minutes.

The couple devoted much time and effort to raising their children. Dinner topics covered world affairs and, like their parents, Janet and David learned to be skilled debaters. The active household usually included a dog and tropical fish. Fall, winter, and spring were spent in Chicago. The family spent summers at their mountain retreat in New England. When Rose's brother also accepted a position to teach in the law school at the University of Chicago, which offered economics courses, the Friedman children became close to their uncle Aaron Director and his wife Katherine, who lived nearby. Friedman and Director often worked hours together in the Friedmans' basement on a variety of carpentry projects. Sometimes they worked at Director's house, because he also had a carpentry shop in his basement.

Upon Friedman's return to the university in 1946, he discovered that little had changed in his eleven-year absence. The economics department still emphasized mathematics and statistics (econometrics) to study economic behavior and conditions. Most of the economics faculty was politically liberal—advocating an extensive role for government in regulating the economy. Frank Knight, who believed in a free-market capitalist economy, was still in the minority. As a result of his teaching and research, however, Friedman's political philosophy was beginning to move in the direction of Frank Knight's. No longer was he "thoroughly Keynesian."

Friedman began teaching price theory and monetary theory (how market prices coordinated economic activity).

Milton Friedman at the University of Chicago. He joined the faculty of the economics department in 1946 and soon won a reputation as an inspired but demanding teacher.

Friedman's brother-in-law, Aaron Director (1901–2004), was a professor at the University of Chicago Law School. Director became known for his work applying economic theories to the study and practice of law.

In the classroom, he demanded that his students come prepared. He had high standards and did not hesitate to give low grades. Friedman believed that sloppy writing meant sloppy thinking, and he spent hours critiquing his students' papers. He avoided the easier-to-grade multiple-choice questions and thus spent hours grading exams requiring written answers. Friedman found grading papers a blow to his self-confidence. "Time and again you find that the students have not really understood what you thought you had made crystal-clear." Helping students learn to make their thoughts and arguments clear would become invaluable to him later in life when communicating economics to the general public.

Blunt, frank, but never cruel or malicious in his comments and criticisms, he mentored many students. In his thirty years at Chicago, he chaired about seventy-five doctoral thesis committees—a task that would require hours of meetings and several readings of each student's dissertation.

Though smoking cigarettes was common and accepted at the time, Friedman forbade smoking in his classroom. Any student daring to be late to class was subjected to a public lesson on negative externalities (imposing costs on others): When you show up late, you impose a cost on everyone in the class; when you don't show up at all, you impose a cost only on yourself. Students quickly learned to arrive to class on time. In the late 1950s, when seventeen graduate students took the written exam for the Ph.D., Friedman passed eight; he failed four and five received a question mark. Yet his classes were filled. Several of the students who took one or more courses from him would become Nobel laureates in economics: James Buchanan (1986), Harry Markowitz (1990), Gary Becker (1992), Robert Lucas (1995), Myron Scholes (1997), and James Heckman (2000).

In addition to teaching, Friedman organized a Workshop in Money and Banking comprised of specially selected graduate students. Occasionally, guest speakers were invited to participate in sessions. Students were admitted to the Workshop with the understanding that they must prepare and present one or more papers to the group. In preparation for each session, all participants had to read in advance the papers or other materials to be discussed. Any participant chronically unprepared risked dismissal.

As a tenured professor, Friedman could have taught his Workshop and classes and gradually phased out researching and publishing, but that was not his nature. An inherently curious man, he desired to learn more about his profession and his profession's role in making society better. Up till now he had researched and written articles in the area of technical economics. But at Chicago he began a transition that would eventually lead him to the study of political philosophy, in part because of the influence of Friedrich Hayek.

Hayek, a professor at the London School of Economics, had gained recognition for, among other things, criticizing Keynesian economic policies. Hayek did not agree with Keynes's theory on government intervention and spending. Instead, he was convinced by Adam Smith's view on the market and spontaneous order. The market was not designed by anyone but evolved in an orderly fashion as individuals coordinated the decisions through market prices. Hayek's views were in the minority, though. Instead, the Keynesian model, which predicted that without extensive government planning the decisions of individuals could result in economic stagnation and persistently high unemployment, prevailed.

Another concern of Hayek's was the spread of socialism. In 1944, he had published *The Road to Serfdom*, a book written to warn the British on the dangers of socialism. It had caught the attention of many Americans as well. Yet socialism had continued to spread. Hayek decided to seek out influential people throughout the world to form a society to combat the socialist threats to freedom and liberty. In 1947, he organized a meeting to be attended by people sympathetic to free markets and limited government. Hayek and Aaron Director had both taught at the London School of Economics, and Hayek invited Director to attend the first international conference. Frank Knight and Friedman were also invited, and the three men sailed to Europe on the *Queen Elizabeth* in the spring.

Thirty-nine attendees met in Mont Pelerin, Switzerland, from April 1–10, 1947. Writing years later on the history of the organization, economist Max Hartwell explained that the members' primary objective was "to halt and reverse current political, social, and economic trends toward socialism." The countries represented included the United States, England, Switzerland, France, Italy, Germany, Norway, Denmark, Belgium, and Sweden. The group was comprised of academicians in economics, law, history, political science, chemistry, and philosophy, as well as three journalists. George Stigler—now a professor at Brown University in Rhode Island—attended also.

At the Hotel du Parc, the participants met and discussed the increasing state control over economic decisions. Two world wars, a catastrophic depression and the perceived failure of capitalism had exacted a toll on the view that a free-market economy was essential to long-run freedom and prosperity. Russia and parts of Germany were socialist countries. China appeared to be next. To the consternation of the conference participants, some influential intellectuals in Europe and the United States were actively involved in spreading communist and socialist ideas.

At the conference, members exchanged opinions on an array of topics, including the importance of a free society and the market economy. In group discussions, members debated a variety of subjects, such as the role of government in a free society. They spent evenings in meetings to organize the new society's structure. They chose officers for president, secretary, and treasurer,

Friedrich von Hayek (center) with students at the London School of Economics, 1948. Hayek, the first president of the Mont Pelerin Society, criticized Keynesian economic policies in his book *The Road to Serfdom*.

and decided that there would be no headquarters, no endowment, and no paid officers or volunteers. The members agreed to pay annual dues.

The purpose was to be that of a society "mainly for the benefit and mutual education of its members," Max Hartwell later recalled. The members agreed that the society would not formulate public policy or become a lobbying group aligned with any political interest group. A heated discussion ensued on what to name this new society. Finally, the members compromised and named the organization for the beautiful location of the inaugural meeting—The Mont Pelerin Society. Ten years would pass before Friedman could attend another meeting. Still, the Society and its members would play an important role in his academic life.

Friedman had maintained ties to the National Bureau of Economic Research, and in 1948 he began a research project with staff member Anna Jacobson Schwartz to study the history of business cycles dating back to the Civil War. Both he and Schwartz had ties to Columbia University, as Schwartz had received her master's degree from Columbia in 1935. For the next seven years, the two would collect and evaluate data tracing the evolution and development of U.S. monetary policy from 1867 to 1960. In all, it would take them more than fifteen years to write and publish a book on their findings.

5 Travel and Theory

After World War II much of Europe had been destroyed, and its economies were in shambles. The U.S. Congress passed the Marshall Plan in 1947 to aid in Europe's economic recovery. In 1950, some of Friedman's former students were instrumental in extending an offer for him to consult at the Marshall Plan Agency in Paris, France. He accepted the job and agreed to work at the Agency during the fall term, after obtaining a leave of absence from teaching at the University of Chicago.

At the end of the summer the Friedmans sailed across the Atlantic Ocean by steamship, and, once settled in Paris, David and Janet were enrolled in a French school. The children did not speak French. Neither David's kindergarten teacher nor Janet's second-grade teacher spoke English. Somehow, using facial expressions and hand signals, the children managed to communicate and soon impressed their parents with how much French they had learned. Whenever possible, the Friedmans took trips to other countries. A car trip to Germany left a lasting impression on them all as they drove through town after town that had experienced the devastating destruction of the wartime bombings.

When Friedman returned to the United States for the January 1951 school term, the Korean War had begun. In December, President Truman had proclaimed a national state of emergency when communist China's entry into the war escalated the conflict.

Friedman was pleased to learn that Friedrich Hayek, the organizer of the first Mont Pelerin Society meeting, had taken a faculty position at the University of Chicago, although not in the economics department,

President Harry S. Truman (left) discusses a U.S. plan to rebuild war-devastated Europe with his advisors: Secretary of State George C. Marshall, Economic Cooperation Administrator Paul G. Hoffman, and Secretary of Commerce Averell Harriman. Under the Marshall Plan—which had been outlined by the secretary of state in a June 1947 speech at Harvard University—the United States provided more than $13 billion in economic and technical assistance to European countries.

but in an interdisciplinary program of study called the Committee on Social Thought. The fifty-one-year-old Hayek held regular seminars, which Friedman frequently attended.

Friedman wrote, "My interest in public policy and political philosophy was rather casual before I joined the faculty of the University of Chicago. Informal discussions with colleagues and friends stimulated a greater interest, which was reinforced by Friedrich Hayek's powerful book *The Road to Serfdom*, by my attendance at the first meeting of the Mont Pelerin Society in 1947, and by discussions with Hayek after he joined the university faculty in 1950." But the greatest influence on Friedman's free-market views during this time was his scholarly work on economic theory.

By the late 1940s, Friedman had become recognized in the economics field for his important contributions to economic analysis. In recognition of his scholarly achievements, thirty-nine-year-old Friedman received the John Bates Clark Medal, a prestigious award given by the American Economic Association every other year to an American economist under the age of forty, in 1951.

Much of Friedman's research pointed to problems he saw with the Keynesian model. Keynes had argued that the economy could stagnate at high rates of unemployment unless the government played an active role in the economy with high levels of government spending. An important concept in the Keynes model was the consumption function, which showed the relationship between income and the amount spent on consumption. Keynes assumed that as income increased so would consumption spending, but that the spending would increase by less than the increase in income. This assumption was plausible since rich people can afford to save a larger percentage of their incomes than can poor people.

But an implication of the Keynesian consumption function is that it will be more difficult to create new jobs as an economy becomes richer. The problem is that consumption spending is by far the biggest source of demand in the economy, and it is growth in demand for goods and services that motivates firms to hire new workers. On the other hand, if the amount consumers want to spend becomes an ever smaller percentage of their incomes, firms will be unwilling to hire the increased number of people looking for jobs in a growing economy. Keynes and his disciples used this stagnation thesis to justify increased government spending to make up for the deficiency in consumer spending.

Of course, some of the spending would be paid for with higher taxes, but the taxes would reduce consumer spending and at least partially offset the positive effect of the additional government spending on employment. Keynes argued that government spending would do more to increase employment if it was paid for with borrowing, which meant running a budget deficit. The result was a strong tendency for government spending to increase, with decisions made by politicians becoming more important on how the country's income was spent, and decisions made by consumers and investors becoming less important.

Recalling his work on consumption expenditures in the 1930s, Friedman thought there was something wrong with the Keynesian consumption function and the stagnation thesis. When he went back and reexamined the data on consumption he found something interesting: It is true that, at any particular time, rich people spend a smaller percentage of their income than do poor people. But Friedman also found that over time consumption spending remained very constant as a percentage of income, showing no tendency to decline.

Friedman developed an explanation for this with what he called the permanent income hypothesis, which says that consumers base their spending on what they expect their long-run, or permanent, income to be, not on what their income is at the moment. People with

By the 1950s, Friedman had begun questioning some of the assumptions of Keynesian economics. His 1957 book, *A Theory of the Consumption Function*, cast doubt on the Keynesian belief in the need for government spending and budget deficits to maintain full employment.

low incomes include many whose incomes are temporarily low (for example, people between jobs, salespeople having a slow month, and novelists between books), and they continue to spend as much as they normally do because they do not expect their permanent incomes to fall. Thus they spend a large percentage of their current income. Similarly, people with high incomes include many with incomes that are only high temporarily, and they do not increase their spending much, if any. Therefore, their spending is a lower percentage of their current income.

Friedman published his ideas in his book *A Theory of the Consumption Function* in 1957. The theoretical and empirical research in this book made an important contribution to economists' understanding of how the economy works. But more important at the time, it generated serious doubt about at least part of the Keynesian argument for the need for government spending, and budget deficits, to maintain full employment. The enthusiasm for Keynesian policies continued, but Friedman had sowed some seeds of doubt in those policies in the minds of many.

In 1953, Friedman accepted a one-year visiting faculty appointment at Gonvill and Caius College at Cambridge University—the university home of the late John Maynard Keynes. The Friedmans first traveled to Italy to attend the August meeting of the International Economic Association. After leaving Italy, they traveled to England where they would live until summer 1954. Once settled in Cambridge, Janet and David were enrolled in school.

The year abroad was enlightening for them all. Friedman and Rose enjoyed their many intellectual discussions with prominent Cambridge economists and some of Keynes's disciples. Janet, age ten and enamored with horses, enjoyed taking riding lessons, and, much to Rose's consternation, began jumping fences. David, age eight, enjoyed reading, especially books by Rudyard Kipling. The family took vacation trips to Switzerland, Germany, Belgium, Holland, Denmark, and Sweden. Rose and Friedman traveled to Madrid, Spain, where he gave two lectures. Almost everywhere the Friedmans traveled a former student or friend of a former student was available to make the visit easier and more pleasant, and England proved no exception. While Friedman and Rose were in Madrid, a former student and his wife took care of Janet and David in Cambridge.

The family took a holiday trip in early summer 1954 to Wales and Scotland. Despite the uncomfortable weather, Friedman and David climbed Ben Nevis in the highlands of Scotland—the highest mountain in the British Isle. In the lowlands of Scotland they visited the gravesite of Adam Smith, the father of political economy. Smith had died in 1790 and his burial site was in a cemetery in Edinburgh. Surprisingly, the family found the site badly neglected. (Some twenty years after this visit, Friedman would be credited with Smith's resurgence in popularity.) The year spent in England had been good for the entire family. The next year, though, would be one of the worst.

In 1955, Friedman was asked by representatives at the International Cooperation Administration—a U.S.

government foreign aid pro-gram—to work in India for three months on a special project. The Indian socialist government was preparing a five-year plan, and the United States government had submitted a request to send a couple of prominent pro-free-market Americans to offer alternative advice to that being offered by social-ist advisors. The request was approved, and Friedman agreed to serve as one of the American advisors.

The eighteenth-century Scottish economist and moral philosopher Adam Smith is considered the father of political economy.

Getting to New Delhi was not an easy task for Friedman; the itinerary included stops in Los Angeles, Tokyo, Hong Kong, Bangkok, and, finally, New Delhi, India. Because commercial airline jets were not yet available, it took him seven days to reach New Delhi from the United States.

Rose and the children had decided to remain in Chicago. Late one night, while the two kids slept in their rooms nearby, Rose was awakened by a man. He wore a mask and held a gun, and he demanded money. But Rose's purse was downstairs. With her mind and body numbed from fright, somehow she managed to climb out of bed and walk down the stairs, the man's hand on her shoulder. Rose pointed at her purse sitting on a bureau. He did not take it. And then "he made a suggestion" that caused her to shriek, she would later recall.

The intruder ran out of the house. Rose ran to an open window and screamed for help until a neighbor rushed over. Her brother, Aaron Director, who lived two blocks away, spent the rest of the night with Rose and the kids. The police came promptly, neighbors searched the area themselves, but the intruder got away. Just three weeks into his three month project, Friedman immediately quit the India project and began the long return to Chicago.

A second tragic event occurred that year when Friedman's mother, Sarah, died at the age of seventy-four. Friedman had remained close to his mother. Summers spent on the East Coast had provided Janet and David regular opportunities to visit their grand-mother and Friedman's two sisters, Tillie and Ruth. Helen, who had generously loaned money to her brother during those lean years in graduate school, had died before Sarah.

The next two years were fairly routine for the Friedman family. The kids attended school; Rose maintained the domestic affairs from their home near the campus; Friedman taught and ran his Workshop at the University of Chicago. Summers continued to be spent at their home in New England, where Friedman concentrated on his research and writing. He and Anna Schwartz had gathered the data for their project—much of which had never before been collected—"tracing the evolution and development of American monetary policy and its consequences for almost a century." Now the data had to be analyzed. This work would result in a book that would have an important influence on economists' understanding of the Great Depression and cast further doubt on the Keynesian model.

Friedman received an invitation to be a Fellow in the Center for Advanced Study in the Behavioral Sciences for 1957–1958. This meant that he could take a hiatus from teaching in windy Chicago and live for a year in sunny Palo Alto, California, the home of Stanford University. It meant he would be paid to work on his research projects in the company of esteemed scientists from the social sciences—including history, sociology, mathematics, biology, and psychiatry. In addition to the better weather, living in California meant that Rose could more easily arrange to visit her parents in Portland and sister Becky in Reno. Friedman accepted the invitation, becoming one of forty-seven Fellows representing thirteen academic disciplines. Janet and David were not as eager to spend a year in California as their parents, though. The promise of a long camping trip upon the family's return to Chicago the next summer helped to change their minds.

At the end of the year Rose and Friedman kept their promise. On the trip home in summer 1958, a carrier was loaded on top of the car with tent and assorted camping gear. The Friedmans found the drive through the desert miserably hot. The car was not air-conditioned, and they stopped and purchased an air cooler— a cylinder filled with water that hung on a window of the car. The air cooler was advertised as a means of keeping the air inside the car cooler than the air outside the car through the process of water evaporation. All one had to do was to pull the string. Unfortunately, the air cooler failed to accomplish much more than to get Rose wet. She would joke years later that whenever she pulled the string, she "got a shower of water." The family was relieved to reach Chicago and cooler weather. Also, great news awaited them.

Despite the earlier rejection and feelings of disappointment, George Stigler had been talked into moving to Chicago to teach economics beginning in fall 1958. The circle of friendship was joined again: Allen Wallis, George Stigler, and Milton Friedman. Friedrich Hayek and Aaron Director were still at Chicago, too. The University of Chicago now had an influential group of free-market proponents on the campus. Their contributions in the areas of economic, political, and human freedom would be significant, although throughout the 1960s and 1970s their views would remain in the minority.

6 Great Books

In 1960, Friedman and Anna Schwartz were nearing the completion of their study on monetary history for the National Bureau of Economic Research (NBER) and were writing a book on their findings—*A Monetary History of the United States 1867–1960*. This book would have a major impact on monetary policy and theory and on how economists thought about the primary cause of the Great Depression.

Popular belief blamed the stock market crash of October 29, 1929, as the primary cause of the Great Depression. But the economy had already started to slow down before the crash (although the crash did not help matters). In fact, the crash did not cause much concern initially, and the federal government did little in response to the crash and the slowdown in the economy. When the economy did not improve and the government finally did intervene, it made matters worse. One of the first misplaced policies enacted was the Smoot-Hawley Tariff, which was passed in June 1930 and greatly increased the tax on imported goods. This legislation significantly increased the prices of imported products consumers bought and imported inputs firms needed to produce products. Also, other countries retaliated with higher tariffs of their own, which hurt their own economies and reduced the amount of goods they bought from America.

The United States economy had experienced depressions before 1929—some of them sharp enough to be referred to as panics. What made the Great Depression notable was not only its severity but that it lasted so long. The economy was still sinking when Franklin Roosevelt became president in March 1933, with the unemployment rate reaching 25 percent and banks failing throughout the country. By this time, many people had become convinced that Karl Marx was right when he predicted that capitalism would collapse.

Few economists were Marxists, however, and although many believed that capitalism was flawed, they also believed that those flaws could be fixed with aggressive government policies. It was the desire to fix capitalism that had motivated Keynes to write his book *The General Theory of Employment, Interest and Money*.

Keynes—who had died in 1946—saw inadequate demand as the fundamental cause of the Depression. His solution to the Depression was for the government to greatly increase spending while keeping taxes low. The spending would not only create more demand directly, but increase incomes earned by workers, who would then spend more of that income, creating more demand, which would create more income and demand, and so on (the Keynesian multiplier effect). Keynes did not attach much significance to the money supply as either the cause or cure of the Depression.

Rather, he thought inadequate demand caused the Depression and was primarily the result of people not spending enough of their income to push the economy forward. Milton Friedman thought differently, however.

When Friedman published *The Theory of the Consumption Function* in 1957, he argued that the economy did not stagnate from people spending a smaller percent of their incomes as the economy grew; thus, there was no reason government had to increase spending for the economy, and personal incomes, to continue growing. By the early 1960s, Friedman was convinced by the research he and Anna Schwartz had done for *A Monetary History* that the major cause of the Great Depression had been a sharp reduction in the nation's money supply. They wrote that "The total stock of money fell by over one-third from 1929 to 1933." When the amount of money falls, people cannot continue buying as much as before without a corresponding fall in prices. But because of price rigidities, it takes quite a while for prices to decline, and they certainly do not drop as fast as the money supply did from 1929 to 1933. Therefore, during the Great Depression, the rapid drop in money caused a corresponding drop in the amount of goods and services being purchased. In addition, government policies were enacted to keep prices from dropping. It was mistakenly thought that higher prices would increase incomes and purchasing power. Instead, these policies served to prolong the Depression caused by the sharp drop in the money supply.

Friedman's research on money cast even more doubt on the arguments of Keynes and his disciples. Friedman became convinced that the Great Depression was not caused by failures of the free-enterprise system that needed to be corrected by government; rather, misguided government policies were responsible. Friedman wrote, "Far from the depression being a failure of the free-enterprise system, it was a tragic failure of government."

The United States Congress had established the Federal Reserve System in 1913 to prevent rapid changes in the money supply. Friedman and Schwartz argued that the Federal Reserve Board could have offset the negative effects of the economic downturn and the bank failures with an expansive monetary policy, and this would have resulted in a short recession instead of the long and deep depression that the country experienced.

By the 1960s, Friedman's research in a number of areas had persuaded him that free markets did a far better job allowing people to solve their own problems than most people realized, and that government attempts to solve people's problems seldom worked as well as most people thought, and often made problems worse. This did not mean that he opposed all government activities: the government was justified in enforcing laws, protecting private property rights, providing national defense, protecting environmental quality, and providing assistance to those suffering from poverty. Yet he believed that even in these activities the government often did a poor job because it relied too much on centralized commands and controls and too little on market-based incentives that gave people more freedom to make their own choices.

Residents of rural Arizona line up for government-provided food handouts, circa 1940. In *A Monetary History of the United States 1867–1960*, Friedman argued that the Great Depression was caused by a shrinking money supply rather than by insufficient demand, and that an expansionary monetary policy would have been a more effective response to the downturn than increased government spending.

Friedman began devoting attention to making his case to a wider audience than professional economists. In a departure from his technical academic publications, he began writing a book for a general audience titled *Capitalism & Freedom* with the help of Rose, while writing *A Monetary History* with Anna Schwartz. Compared to the eight hundred pages in the technical book filled with graphs and charts that Friedman and Schwartz wrote, *Capitalism & Freedom* is short, approximately two hundred pages. The book covers contemporary public policy issues explaining Friedman's views on the role of government in a free society, controlling money, foreign trade, taxation, income distribution, and poverty. Two major topics include Friedman's views on the military draft and the voucher system for improving education in America. The all-volunteer military and the voucher system would become two of Milton Friedman's most significant contributions to public policy.

Friedman did not believe that a free society should force young men into military service with a draft, and he used *Capitalism & Freedom* to put forth his argument to the general public. In Chapter Two, "The Role of Government in a Free Society," he writes: "The appropriate free market arrangement is volunteer military forces; which is to say, hiring men to serve." Friedman's argument for a volunteer military was twofold. First and foremost, the draft violated the freedom of young men to make their own choice on serving in the military given their personal circumstances and preferences. Second, the volunteer military was cheaper than the draft. Friedman was not against young men and women serving in the military, but he believed that the government should pay enough to get them to choose military service over their alternatives. This would be cheaper than the draft because those with less valuable alternatives, as determined by them, would tend to join the military. Under the draft, most young men, even those with very valuable alternatives (high opportunity cost), are forced into the military. The taxpayers pay less under a draft, but their savings are more than offset by the higher opportunity costs of those who are drafted.

Regarding education in America, Friedman argued that because of a lack of competition, the current system of public education was archaic compared to the many advances made in other areas, including industry and technology. For this reason, he believed that many public schools were doing a poor job educating students, particularly public schools in poor neighborhoods. Friedman pointed out that government could finance public education without providing it. Government could pay for education by giving parents educational vouchers that they could use at the public or private schools of their choice for their children's education. If parents had that choice, "Competition would force the government schools to shape up or close down," he argued. Improving the education system would become one of Friedman and Rose's biggest causes, and they would establish the Milton and Rose D. Friedman Foundation to promote public understanding and support for parental choice in education.

Capitalism & Freedom, published in 1962 by the University of Chicago Press, is dedicated "To Janet and David and their contemporaries who must carry the torch of liberty on its next lap." The major academic journals reviewed the book but the popular press showed little interest. Only one major newsweekly, the *Economist*, published in London, reviewed the book. Yet the book became an international success. As of 2006, the book was still in print with nearly 1 million copies sold.

Wanderjahr

David Friedman enrolled at Harvard University in 1962. That same year Janet transferred from Bryn Mawr College in Pennsylvania to the University of California at Berkeley. With the children grown and *Capitalism & Freedom* completed, Friedman and Rose decided to embark on an around-the-world wanderjahr—a German word for a year of wandering. The trip had two purposes: to allow Friedman to study monetary conditions of various countries and to celebrate his and Rose's twenty-fifth wedding anniversary in July 1963. Friedman, always money-conscious, secured funding for the wanderjahr by obtaining fellowships from the Ford Foundation and the Carnegie Corporation. On August 29, 1962, he and Rose boarded the *Queen Elizabeth* in New York. Janet and David stood on the dock and waved good-bye.

Their first stop was the port in Cherbourg, France. From there they traveled to Paris by train. They stayed in a modestly priced hotel for three days making further travel arrangements and visiting friends. The Friedmans walked the city—a "favorite pastime in Paris," Rose later recalled. Also, they saw an opera and Paris's famous Folies Bergères. From Paris they traveled to Knokke,

Belgium, to attend a Mont Pelerin Society meeting. From Belgium they traveled to Warsaw, Poland, a communist country, where they received their "first real introduction to communism," Friedman said years later.

Friedman had promised to write a paper for the Radio Free Europe station in West Berlin, and he finished the paper in Warsaw. Knowing that mail was inspected in many communist countries, he used the telephone in his motel room and called the U.S. Embassy. Friedman requested that a diplomatic pouch be sent to his room to send a confidential document to West Berlin. An embassy representative brusquely informed Friedman that such a request was impossible. It was against the rules. Before hanging up, he asked Friedman where he was staying. Not long after the call, a man knocked on the Friedmans' hotel room door. Without ever speaking one word, the American handed Friedman an identification card. Friedman would write that the American "looked around the room, stationed himself with his back against the wall under a ventilation grille, pointed to it, and conveyed by sign language that it was probably bugged. He then gestured for me to give him what I had." With Friedman's package in hand, the man departed in silence.

In Poland, they joined a guided bus tour traveling to Moscow, the capital city of the Soviet Union, and the bus broke down on the Poland-Russia border. Official documents authorizing the bus to be towed across the border for repair were not available, but for the passengers to get to their next destination, the bus had to be on the Russian side of the border. Refusing to give up, the adventuresome passengers disembarked and pushed the bus the short distance into Russia. The trip still appeared to be in jeopardy when the guide could not locate a towing service. After some delay, the passengers made a transaction with the driver of a passing cattle truck to tow the bus to a nearby town for repair.

The next obstacle they faced was a place to stay. In the small Russian border town, there were no hotels designated for tourists. Fortunately, the guide managed to obtain some rooms in a hotel for residents of Russia. Unfortunately, the rooms were filthy, and only one room had a bathtub for the passengers to share. Some of the younger women on the tour purchased cleaning products, and they scoured the tub.

During their tour of the Russian countryside, Friedman and Rose quickly learned to find the public toilets by smell. Roads in the rural countryside generally were unpaved; paved roads were for military vehicles only.

They discovered life in the city of Moscow much different than life in the small towns, in part because of the government's willingness to spend state money to impress foreign tourists. And yet, the wide gap between affluence and poverty was readily apparent. The Friedmans thought the new, glistening buildings, such as the Palace of the Soviets, a disturbing contrast to the dull and drab retail shops. They learned that few people could afford to buy a car. And, except on rainy days, those cars they saw did not have windshield wipers; these were hidden, locked inside the automobiles to protect them from being stolen.

A view of Moscow's famous Red Square, which the Friedmans visited in 1962. The Kremlin, where the Soviet Union's government had its offices, is the large building on the left.

Friedman and Rose felt that they were constantly watched in Moscow. A loudspeaker in their hotel room regularly spouted communist propaganda, even at night. During the visit, Friedman attempted to obtain data on the currency and coins issued by the Soviet Union's central bank—data easily obtainable in the United States. He was unsuccessful. Economists at the U.S. Embassy informed him that such figures "were a state secret," he later recalled.

Friedman and Rose gladly left Moscow and flew to Belgrade, Yugoslavia. In Belgrade, they learned that not all communist countries are alike, just as not all democratic countries are alike. The people walking the streets appeared to be more tastefully dressed than those they saw in Moscow. There was no noisy loudspeaker in their hotel room to keep them awake at night. In contrast to what they had observed in the Soviet Union, food in

Belgrade was readily available and cheap. Throughout the wanderjahr, he and Rose made an effort to speak to people on the streets and to take side trips to rural areas to observe how people outside the cities lived. In general, they found the people they met on the city streets of Belgrade much friendlier than those in Moscow.

Also, Friedman asked for and received data from Yugoslavia's central bank. Dr. Dimitrijevic, who knew one of Friedman's former students and was familiar with Friedman's articles on money, assisted Friedman in his research. Friedman gave several talks at the bank on monetary theory and policy. In later years, several Yugoslavian economists would visit the University of Chicago and participate in his Money and Banking Workshop. Dr. Dimitrijevic would spend the 1969 winter quarter in the Chicago economics department as a visiting scholar.

Next, Friedman and Rose traveled to Israel. Because both spoke Yiddish, they expected to learn much more about the Israeli people and their customs than they had learned in Poland, Russia, or Yugoslavia. They were disappointed when a former student serving as the Friedmans' guide warned them not to speak Yiddish. At the moment, Yiddish was unpopular; Hebrew, which neither Friedman spoke, was the official language of Israel. Rose wrote, "Though we were not observant Jews, we had expected to feel at home in Israel. Instead we felt less at home than in England or France. The combination of a foreign language of which we were entirely ignorant and the faces of the Oriental Jews, which were so different from the European Jews whom we were familiar with, made Israel seem very foreign."

Friedman gave a number of talks and two seminars. At the Bank of Israel, he continued his study of money. Weekends consisted of sightseeing trips to various parts of the country, and former students were available to assist as guides. Rose found some of her mother's relatives living in Israel. The visit went well, and in future trips the Friedmans always made plans to see them.

The Friedmans flew to Munich, Germany, the week before Christmas 1962. There they met Janet and David for a skiing trip in Austria. Following the Christmas vacation, they would not see each other again until June.

The next wanderjahr stop was Greece, where Friedman conducted his research at the central bank and the Institute for Economic Research in Athens. Once again, former students volunteered to serve as research assistants and guides. From Greece, the Friedmans continued to India.

Friedman and Rose were met at the Bombay airport in late morning and taken to the luxurious Taj Mahal Hotel, where a reception committee waited to greet them. Once the welcoming speeches concluded, the Friedmans were shown to a suite. Exhausted from the long flight, they spent the remainder of the day and night catching up on their sleep. While in India, they visited New Delhi. John Kenneth Galbraith was America's ambassador to India. Though Galbraith was a well-known Harvard economist, and held what Friedman would say later were "sharply different political views," the two had yet maintained a friendship for many years. Friedman and Rose visited the embassy, where they enjoyed lunch with Galbraith and his wife.

Rose and Milton Friedman on skiing trip in Austria, 1962.

India had obtained its independence from Great Britain in 1947. The new government of India had subsequently adopted the Soviet Union's central planning model for directing the economy. The Friedmans toured factories and talked to academics, journalists, and business owners to learn more about central planning in India. In their travels they observed that the roads were in poor condition, and many were not paved. They encountered numerous beggars. Many of the Indian people used bicycles to traverse the city streets and the rural countryside. While they saw many new buildings in cities such as Bombay and New Delhi, Friedman viewed them as a sign of waste, not of progress, because of the severe poverty they observed. "On every side, there were extremes of unrelieved poverty that are difficult to make credible to someone who has not been to India," he observed.

Friedman and Rose thought the infrastructure and conditions in Bombay (known today as Mumbai), New Delhi, and the nearby localities bad, and the conditions in Calcutta (today's Kolkata) deplorable. The couple arrived in Calcutta on March 26, 1963. They had planned to stay until April 6, but after two days they left. Rose would later recall that "nearly a tenth of the population had no home other than the street—they ate, slept, and defecated on the street. The filth and stench were worse than we have ever experienced either before our visit or since and the poverty and begging was even more intensive than in the other places we had visited so we decided that we would move on."

En route to Japan they made stops in Bangkok, Thailand; Siem Reap, Cambodia; Saigon (modern-day Ho Chi Minh City) in southern Vietnam; and Hong Kong. They found Bangkok hot and humid. In Cambodia they spent a few pleasant days visiting impressive ruins and Buddhist temples in Siem Reap and Angkor Wat. Surprisingly, with all the fighting that had occurred for decades in the nearby country of Vietnam, Cambodia had somehow remained neutral. Unfortunately, neutrality and peace would end during the 1970s, and the country would be taken over by a communist regime.

Their visit to Saigon, the capital city of South Vietnam, was unremarkable, despite the fact that the region had been at war for decades. Before World War II, Vietnam had been a French colony, but after that war ended in 1945, Vietnamese communists led by Ho Chi Minh fought for independence from France. After a disastrous French defeat at the Battle of Dien Bien Phu in May 1954, French leaders agreed to a settlement, the Geneva Accords, in which two countries, North and South Vietnam, were established. North Vietnam was led by a communist government, and was supported by the Soviet Union and China. The United States provided financial aid and military assistance to the anti-communist government of South Vietnam, led by Ngo Dinh Diem.

During the late 1950s, an insurgency threatened the government of South Vietnam. The Vietcong were communists who lived in South Vietnam and wanted to overthrow Diem's regime. The government of North Vietnam provided supplies and military assistance to aid the Vietcong's guerrilla war in the South. By the time Milton and Rose visited South Vietnam in 1963, there were about 15,000 American soldiers in Vietnam, many of them stationed in or around the capital city, where they served as advisors to the South Vietnamese military. It "seemed like an American army base," Rose said later.

In January 1965, little more than a year after the Friedmans' visit, the U.S. government sharply increased the number of American soldiers in Vietnam. By the end of that year, nearly 200,000 U.S. troops were engaged in combat with the Vietcong and the North Vietnamese Army (NVA); by 1968, more than 500,000 American soldiers were fighting in Vietnam. The war turned out to be a disastrous quagmire for U.S. forces. The United States remained engaged until 1973, when the last U.S. combat troops were withdrawn from the country; two years later, South Vietnam was conquered by the communist North.

The Friedmans left Vietnam and flew to Hong Kong, where they discovered that Hong Kong lived up to its reputation as "a shoppers' paradise," Rose said. It was a free-market paradise, also. Although Hong Kong was then a colony of Great Britain, its government had a great deal of autonomy in regulating the economy. Unlike the British United Kingdom, Hong Kong had no tariffs on imports or exports. They spent a week or more resting, relaxing, and studying one of the most unique economic systems in the world. In 1995, Hong Kong would be "rated first" for economic freedom out of over one hundred countries, Friedman would write. On July 1, 1997, in fulfillment of an agreement dating back to the nineteenth century, Hong Kong would become part of China; however, the communist Chinese government would promise to allow Hong Kong to keep its economic autonomy.

Upon their arrival in Tokyo, Japan, the Friedmans were met by a welcoming committee. At their welcoming reception in India, the couple had received flowers. In Japan, to Rose's surprise, only Friedman received flowers. They appreciated the Japanese people's unique customs, including bowing to family members and friends to show respect. The Friedmans thought the public and private gardens they visited—meticulously pruned by hundreds of workers—most impressive. Unlike other countries visited the past few months, they could drink the water in Japan without fear of getting a stomach illness. They experienced Tokyo's ethnic diversity, and found the Japanese people especially friendly.

Friedman conducted his research on money with cooperation from the Bank of Japan. He gave talks and expanded his network of friends, some of whom would become members of the Mont Pelerin Society. Janet and David joined their parents, and on June 25, 1963, Friedman and Rose celebrated twenty-five years of marriage. The family took a vacation cruise from Japan to Singapore with stops in Hong Kong and Manila. From Singapore they flew to the island of Bali, and from Bali they flew to Kuala Lumpur, where Janet and David had fun snorkeling and swimming. Friedman, when not recreating with the family, gave talks and did further research. The next stop was Taiwan, and then they returned to Japan for a few more days of sightseeing. In July, they left Japan by ship and sailed to Honolulu, Hawaii. After a few days enjoying the islands, the wanderjahr ended with a flight back to the West Coast.

The one-year around-the-world trip was a great success. In addition to gathering information and data on monetary conditions in other countries and giving talks to spread the word on the value of a market economy in promoting political and economic freedom, the trip was a success because of the many friendships made. In later years, the Friedmans would return to some of the cities visited during their wanderjahr and renew friendships. These friendships would become especially beneficial to them in future endeavors, both scientifically and personally.

8 Public Figure

riedman and Rose were happy to be home again, although almost immediately he found himself embroiled in a storm of controversy because of his book with Anna Schwartz. Throughout the trip Friedman and Schwartz had exchanged letters concerning the publication of their book *A Monetary History*. The magnum opus, which had taken fifteen years to write, was published in 1963.

Throughout his years of research on monetary theory and history, Friedman had been criticizing Keynesian economics in articles and in speeches. But publication of the book provoked the greatest outburst of protest among Keynesian economists, by providing evidence that the Great Depression was primarily the result of a collapse in the money supply that government policy allowed. Their research in *A Monetary History* also indicated that, as opposed to Keynesian economics, the best way to reduce economic fluctuations, with periods of depression followed by periods of inflation, was for the Federal Reserve to maintain a moderate growth in the money supply of about 2 to 3 percent per year—roughly equal to the average growth rate in economic output.

By the late 1960s, Friedman's ideas had begun to supplant the Keynesian model. In 1967, Friedman was elected president of the American Economic Association.

Friedman believed that with such predictable growth in the money supply, natural adjustments in a market economy would quickly bring an economy out of a downturn in a recession, and prevent inflation during economic growth. *A Monetary History* was as much about inflation as about recessions and depressions, and indicated strongly that the cause of inflation (a persistent increase in the general price level) was the result of money increasing more rapidly than the growth in goods and services. Friedman famously said "Inflation is always and everywhere a monetary phenomenon."

Keynes's disciples thought that changes in aggregate demand were the critical factor in both the unemployment that accompanied recessions and the general price increases of inflation. According to Keynesians, unemployment was caused by too little demand and inflation was caused by too much demand. From the early 1960s into the 1970s, Keynesian economics was widely accepted by economists and politicians, with economists becoming more important advising presidents, and other government officials, on how to fine-tune the economy with the right mix of government spending and taxation. For example, economists advised that during unemployment the federal government should increase spending and reduce taxes, which would increase aggregate demand, stimulate a return to economic growth, and lower unemployment. During inflation, spending should be reduced and taxes increased, which would reduce aggregate demand and lower inflation.

While Keynesian ideas provided some political justification for increased political spending, many politicians tended to forget the Keynesian recommendation for reducing spending and increasing taxes during inflation, as that typically proved politically unpopular.

Many Keynesian politicians and economists resisted Friedman's ideas supporting steady growth in the money supply and letting market adjustments stabilize the economy, and some criticized Friedman personally. He was referred to as, among other things, "a heretic, a Rasputin, or a numskull, or some combination of all three."

Despite the controversy, Friedman's contribution to economic history and theory could not be denied, and he continued to receive honors from his colleagues, if somewhat grudgingly from many. He was elected to serve as the 1967 President of the American Economic

Association, and was in constant demand as a speaker before academic and business audiences. His ideas were slowly being accepted by an increasing number of economists as his Ph.D. students were achieving prominence in the profession through their writings and teaching. In addition, beginning in the 1970s, economic events added support for Friedman's theories and cast further doubt on Keynes's. The most important event was the onset of what became known as stagflation—both increasing inflation and unemployment at the same time. Keynesian economics had no reasonable explanation for this.

The Keynesian position on inflation and unemployment was illustrated by the Phillips Curve, which showed a trade-off between inflation and unemployment. The Phillips Curve is named after A.W. Phillips, who published an article in 1958 which used historical data from Britain to show that the higher money wages were associated with lower unemployment. This curve was soon adapted by economists to show that higher inflation rates were associated with lower unemployment. This result seemed to support the Keynesian argument that more aggregate demand led to more inflation and lower unemployment, and that less aggregate demand led to lower inflation but more unemployment.

Then in the 1970s, economists noticed that the Phillips Curve for the United States and other countries was shifting out, showing that both inflation and unemployment were increasing at the same time. This could not be explained by the Keynesian economic model, which saw unemployment and inflation moving in different directions in response to changes in aggregate demand. Milton Friedman, however, had an explanation. In his presidential address before the American Economic Association in 1967, he explained how his economic theory based on the importance of changes in the money supply could easily account for how both inflation and unemployment might increase (or how they might both decrease or move in opposite directions) at the same time.

Friedman argued that the first effect of increasing the money supply would be to make people feel wealthier, and result in the purchase of more goods and services. This increased demand would increase profits and

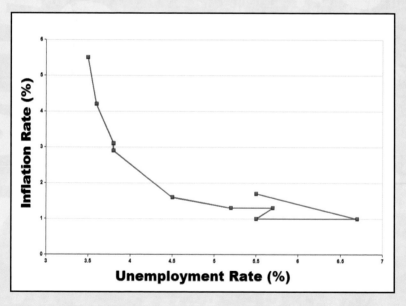

The Phillips Curve, an economic model first proposed in 1958, indicates a relationship between the rate of inflation and the unemployment rate. The chart above shows the curve's effect in the United States from 1960 to 1969; each dot represents an annual average. During the late 1960s, Friedman argued that the Phillips Curve model was too simple to explain the complex factors that cause inflation to increase.

motivate firms to expand output and hire more workers, thus reducing unemployment. It would take a year or so for the increased money supply to cause a rise in inflation—a general increase in the level of prices—according to the historical evidence presented by Friedman and Schwartz in *A Monetary History*. So far, the argument was consistent with the Phillips Curve; that is, more inflation would cause less unemployment.

Unfortunately, the reduction in unemployment was only temporary, according to Friedman. Once inflation increased, people would soon realize that the increased money supply did not increase their wealth. They had more money, but that was offset by the higher prices. Consequently, consumers reduced the amount of goods and services they were willing to buy and the unemployment rate went back up to about where it was before. Inflation was higher, but the unemployment rate was now no lower than before.

Friedman pointed out that it was possible to prevent a return to the original unemployment level but only temporarily, by further, and more rapid, increases in the money supply, which meant even higher inflation. Only by increasing inflation by more than consumers and businesses expected, could expanding the money supply keep people buying more and keep unemployment lower than normal. But people would eventually recognize what was happening and unemployment would go back up as inflation was increasing. Indeed, because inflation caused distortions in the economy—in particular, reducing investment—by making it difficult for people to know what the future value of money would be, increasing

A long line outside the unemployment office, Detroit, Michigan, January 1980. Stagflation—high unemployment and high inflation—bedeviled the U.S. economy in the 1970s. Friedman had anticipated the situation.

inflation would soon cause the unemployment rate to rise higher than the normal level. This is what was happening from the mid-1960s until the late 1970s and, as Friedman predicted in the 1960s, both inflation and unemployment were rising by the middle of the 1970s.

By the late 1970s, the Keynesians were very much on the defensive. Keynesian economics was not dead—it still provided some insights into the short-run effects of some economic policies—but it was no longer the dominant view among economists. John Kenneth Galbraith (a lifelong Keynesian despite his friendship with Friedman) said, "the age of John Maynard Keynes gave way to the age of Milton Friedman."

Friedman's work was not finished. He continued to devote time and effort to his scholarship and advancing the frontiers of economic knowledge. In addition, he expanded his role of public figure by writing more for the general public and advising politicians on public policy. And the public had begun to take notice.

Friedman was offered an opportunity to serve as an economic adviser for the 1964 Republican presidential nominee, Barry Goldwater. Although Friedman's political preference was libertarian (one who advocates a minimal government and a primary reliance on free markets) rather than Republican or Democrat, he agreed to assist on the condition that he not be involved in campaigning. Goldwater, a U.S. senator from Arizona, had little chance of winning the presidential campaign. President Lyndon Johnson, who had assumed the presidency upon John F. Kennedy's assassination, defeated Goldwater by a wide margin.

In 1966, an editor at Newsweek magazine asked Friedman to become a regular columnist. The column would rotate among three prominent economists—Paul Samuelson, Henry Wallich, and Milton Friedman. Newsweek wanted the opinion column to represent the liberal, center, and conservative ideological views, and Friedman was contacted to provide the conservative, free-market perspective. Friedman had reservations, fearing that writing a triweekly column would interfere with his research projects. Rose, on the other hand, encouraged him, saying that "research findings were barren if they were not communicated to the public." David agreed with his mother. Nor would Friedman be the first economist to write for both professional economists and the public—John Maynard Keynes and Kenneth Galbraith had both written articles for public consumption.

Still, Friedman hesitated. He spoke to his colleagues and friends, including George Stigler. Stigler, too, encouraged him to accept the assignment. All agreed that the column would offer another means, in addition to *Capitalism & Freedom*, of explaining to the public the importance of economic and political freedom. Friedman accepted on one condition: he wanted final approval of the content. The editor agreed. Friedman would write the column for eighteen years.

The *Newsweek* column did more than anything else to introduce Milton Friedman to the public and to politicians. Richard Nixon (whom Friedman had previously met through Allen Wallis) was the Republican presidential candidate in the 1968 election, and he won a narrow victory over Hubert Humphrey, the Democratic candidate.

An incoming president often has a short honeymoon with Congress in which to get new public policy initiatives passed or old public policies changed. To take advantage of this honeymoon period, presidential candidates organize committees to strategize and develop legislative initiatives, and Friedman was recruited to join Nixon's advisory group on the economy. George Shultz, dean of the School of Business at the University of Chicago and an expert labor negotiator, also agreed to serve. Friedman's recommendations for new initiatives included a proposal he had introduced in

Milton Friedman served as an economic advisor to Richard Nixon during his 1968 presidential campaign.

Capitalism & Freedom: ending the draft and instituting an all-volunteer army.

After Nixon was sworn in as the thirty-seventh President, he appointed Friedman to an advisory commission to study the all-volunteer army. The fifteen-member commission was widely split at the beginning, but after more than two hundred hours of taking testimony and discussion, the commission made a unanimous recommendation to end the draft, and on January 27, 1973, Congress did so. Friedman would write that "No public-policy activity that I have ever engaged in has given me as much satisfaction as the All-Volunteer Commission."

Friedman made the cover of *Time* magazine in the December 19, 1969, issue. The article on Friedman titled "The Intellectual Provocateur" stated that "Friedman is a man totally devoted to ideas—isolating them in pure form, expressing them in uncompromising terms and following them wherever they may lead. His basic philosophy is simple and unoriginal: personal freedom is the supreme good—in economic, political and social relations."

Years of practice and experience had made Friedman a writer who could take complex economic concepts and make them comprehendible to someone with no economic training. And, even though he did not make the finals in the National Oratorical Contest on the U.S. Constitution as a child, at age fifty-seven he had obtained a national reputation as a superb debater. He was also a highly skilled lecturer in the classroom and was in great demand as a public speaker. The esteem Milton Friedman had earned as an academic economist in the 1960s was beginning to be accompanied in the 1970s by the esteem he held as a public figure.

In 1972, two significant events occurred that affected Friedman and Rose personally. Janet, who had married and lived in California, gave birth to the Friedman's first grandson, Richard Kyle Stansby, on July 4. Second, Friedman, sixty years old and still physically active, began suffering from pains in his chest. Friedman's

Army recruits receive their clothing allotment as they arrive at a basic training facility, 1977. Friedman's work for President Nixon's All-Volunteer Commission resulted in the end of the military draft in 1973. Since then, America's military services have been composed of volunteers.

father had died from heart trouble at forty-nine. Worried, Friedman went to see a doctor, and his pains were diagnosed as angina. He began a treatment of medication, but it proved unsuccessful.

Because he was the president of the Mont Pelerin Society, Friedman attended the annual meeting in Montreux, Switzerland, and gave his presidential address on "The Jews and Capitalism." Soon after his return, Friedman and Rose went to the Mayo Clinic in Rochester, Minnesota, for tests. Many hospitals had not yet purchased the equipment to detect blood circulation through the arteries. Bypass surgery was relatively new. The Mayo Clinic had both the equipment for conducting tests and the surgeons to perform bypass surgery.

The results of Friedman's angiogram test showed a blocked artery. The doctors did not believe the condition to be life-threatening at the time and advised him to wait on surgery. But Friedman did not want to live with the worry that one day his condition would suddenly worsen and cause a stroke or heart attack. He chose to undergo bypass surgery. Following surgery there were complications from internal bleeding and a second operation was performed to stop the bleeding. Once released from the hospital, he and Rose spent two months recuperating in Palm Springs, Florida. Finally, in early 1973, he felt well enough to resume a busy schedule.

Friedman's popularity as a public figure continued to grow. He was so busy he had to turn down some of the invitations he received to travel and give speeches. He appeared on television shows, including *Meet the Press* and the *Donahue Show*. Even *Playboy* magazine contacted Friedman regarding an interview. Initially, he did not want to get involved with a magazine known for nudity. When further investigation revealed that the magazine contained articles with intellectual content, he finally agreed to the interview. The article appeared in the February 1973 issue, and Friedman was pleasantly surprised with both the article and the positive response it received. Usually, he enjoyed the perks that came with being a public figure, but he would soon learn that it had a downside.

Chile had elected a Marxist, Salvador Allende, as its president in 1970. Before long, the country began suffering serious economic problems under Allende's socialist policies, and he died when his government was overthrown in a military coup led by General Augusto Pinochet in September 1973. Pinochet was successful in suppressing political opponents—many died or went missing—but he knew little about how to solve the economic problems of inflation and shortages that the Chilean people faced. A group of Chilean economists (former University of Chicago Department of Economics students) were prepared with a plan. They submitted their plan for economic recovery based on free-market principles to important military generals in the new regime, but nothing happened, at least at first, until the Chilean economy worsened.

General Pinochet then appointed several of the Chicago-educated economists to key leadership positions in his government. Professor Al Harberger at the University of Chicago had maintained close ties to the

General Augusto Pinochet led a bloody coup that overthrew the democratically elected government of Salvador Allende in Chile. In the aftermath of the September 1973 coup, Pinochet's regime tortured and murdered thousands of Chileans. Milton Friedman drew the ire of human-rights advocates when he briefly met with Pinochet in 1975 to discuss Chile's economic problems.

Chilean economists. Harberger was asked to travel to Chile in early 1975 at the invitation of the Banco Hipotecario (a Chilean bank) to assess the country's economic conditions and to recommend solutions. Harberger invited Friedman and a student in the doctoral program to go with him. Rose went too. While in Chile the men gave some seminars and public lectures. In Friedman's opinion, the primary problem was inflation, and he had no qualms about telling the Chileans so, or in lecturing on the importance of a free society.

The American economists received an invitation to meet with General Pinochet. In the forty-five minute meeting they talked to General Pinochet—communicating through interpreters—about the economy. At the conclusion of the meeting, General Pinochet asked Friedman to submit a letter formally explaining the country's economic conditions and solutions to ending the inflationary depression. In the letter dated April 21, 1975, Friedman wrote, "The key economic problems of Chile are clearly twofold: inflation, and the promotion of a healthy social market economy. The two problems are related—the more effectively you can invigorate the free private market, the lower will be the transitional costs of ending inflation." He then recommended a shock approach to improving the economy: a drastic cut in the money supply growth.

On September 21, 1975, the *New York Times* published an article branding Friedman as a personal advisor to General Pinochet and his administration. Articles in international newspapers—Britain, France, Germany, and Canada—condemned Friedman for supporting "a fascist military junta that allegedly took delight in torturing people," he recalled. The University of Chicago student newspaper, *Chicago Maroon*, attacked Professor Friedman and called for a protest in the quadrangle in front of the administration building. The university president quickly intervened and managed to get the planned protest cancelled. Friedman and Rose, who had sold their big home and moved into an apartment, were heckled by a few protesters picketing in front of their building.

Friedman did not know whether to be mad or amused by the allegations, since he had not been attacked previously when he gave economic advice to socialist governments that were as brutal as the Pinochet regime, if not more so. After all, giving advice to a government did not indicate approval of that government's policies. Furthermore, Al Harberger, the organizer of the trip to Chile, was not attacked in the media. Friedman wondered if he had been singled out because of his connection to Goldwater and Nixon and because of the *Newsweek* columns. Being well-known definitely had a price.

The Chilean government did introduce some free-market reform policies—a partial shock treatment. And, as Friedman had predicted, the country's economy worsened temporarily. However, as he had also predicted, one year later, as consumer expectations began to adjust to a slower rate of price rises, growth resumed. The economy began to improve. Unfortunately, Pinochet continued to be a cruel dictator, who had little use for human rights and freedom. Under his rule, some 3,200 people were executed or disappeared, and as many as 30,000 more were tortured or exiled.

In fall 1974, the Friedmans received some exciting news: Friedrich Hayek, the tireless advocate of capitalism and freedom, was awarded the Nobel Prize. Friedman was becoming more optimistic that Keynesianism, while still a dominant view in the opinion of some economists, was weakening.

The year 1976 was another milestone in the Friedmans' life, both personally and professionally. During the summer, Friedman and Rose visited David, his wife, and their new baby boy, Patri, in Blacksburg,

Virginia. Although David had completed a Ph.D. at the University of Chicago in physics, he had joined the faculty at Virginia Tech as a professor of economics. His office was in the Center for Public Choice, founded by a University of Chicago graduate in economics, Professor James Buchanan. (Dr. Buchanan would win the Nobel Prize in 1986.) Sadly, soon after the visit, David and his wife separated and divorced. She and Patri moved to Chicago.

The second significant event occurred on October 14, 1976. Friedman flew to Detroit, Michigan, early in the morning. The Michigan legislature was considering a proposal, Proposition C, to enact an amendment that would establish a cap on how much the state government could spend. Friedman was part of a group meeting to strategize on a campaign to get this amendment passed. Arriving in Detroit, Friedman was surprised by the number of photographers and reporters awaiting his arrival. One reporter rushed up to Friedman in the parking lot wanting an interview with the Nobel Prize award winner, while another shouted a question at Friedman, asking if winning the Nobel Prize was the pinnacle of his career. Astounded to learn he had received the prestigious award, Friedman replied with his typical blunt candor that the true judge of his theories would be the opinion of the economics profession on his work after it had been thoroughly analyzed and met the test of time (in twenty-five to fifty years), not the opinion of a Nobel Prize committee.

9 Nobel Laureate

riedman and Rose hastily prepared to attend the December award ceremonies in Stockholm, Sweden. In addition, they made plans to move. After thirty years, Friedman was retiring as a professor of economics at the University of Chicago. He and Rose were moving to California in January 1977, the year of his sixty-fifth birthday.

Winning a Nobel award brings immediate worldwide recognition. Winning the prize is not only a boon for the award recipient, but for his or her institution of affiliation as well. In 1976, the University of Chicago had two Nobel award recipients: Saul Bellow (literature) and Milton Friedman (economics). Having had award winners in the past, the administration at Chicago knew what to expect, and it immediately made plans to send representatives to attend the ceremonies in Sweden. The *Chicago Tribune* was sending a reporter and photographer to cover the events. Chicago television stations were sending film crews. Neither Janet nor David could attend, but a few close friends were going.

Unfortunately, a few unwanted people also were planning to attend. Friedman had already experienced some of the highly organized protests of the anti-Pinochet groups. Now a Nobel laureate, Friedman was an even bigger target.

Once again he was criticized in newspapers. Four of the 1976 Nobel laureates publicly denounced the choice of Milton Friedman as an award recipient. Friedman, with assistance from friends, repeatedly attempted to get the facts published and discredit the attackers. He gave a press conference. Still, the protests continued. Because the organizers of the Nobel awards ceremony and ancillary events received advance warning that anti-Pinochet groups would be demonstrating in Stockholm, Friedman and Rose were introduced to bodyguards upon arriving at the Stockholm airport on Monday, December 6. Each would have a bodyguard during the week of festivities, twenty-four hours a day.

Many different congratulatory events were held in addition to the main ceremony to honor the award recipients. U.S. Ambassador David Smith and his wife hosted the Friedmans at a luncheon. The Friedmans attended a dinner hosted by the Stockholm Club of Economics, where Friedman gave a brief talk.

Alfred Nobel, the Swedish inventor of dynamite, had been an astute business man. He died on December 10, 1896, and in his will he had left money and instructions for the creation of five awards to be given annually to distinguished men and women who had made significant contributions in physics, chemistry, medicine, literature, and peace. In the 1960s, the Central Bank of Sweden established the Nobel Memorial Prize in Economics, to add to those prizes created by Alfred Nobel. The first Nobel Memorial Prize in Economics—officially known as the Sveriges Riksbank Prize in Economic Sciences in Memory of Alfred Nobel—was awarded jointly to Jan Tinbergen and Ragnar Frisch in 1969.

The Nobel Prizes are prestigious because of the rigorous screening that takes place in selecting the world's best scientists, scholars, writers, and contributors to peace. In some cases a prize, and the generous monetary gift, is shared among two or more winners. In recent years, an award recipient has received nearly $1 million. A prize is not given posthumously, unless an award recipient dies after he or she has been notified. The selection process is secretive, and unsuccessful nominees cannot be identified for fifty years. Why some people are nominated and others not is unclear; for

Milton and Rose Friedman at the Nobel ball, 1976.

example, Joseph Stalin, secretary general of the Communist Party of the Soviet Union, was twice nominated and never received a Nobel Prize. Mahatma Gandhi—a symbol of nonviolence in the twentieth century—was nominated several times between 1937 and 1948 and never received the Peace Prize. All awards but the Peace Prize are presented at a ceremony in Stockholm, Sweden. The Peace Prize is presented at a ceremony in Oslo, Norway.

On the Friday afternoon of December 10, 1976, Friedman and Rose and their bodyguards rode by car in rain and darkness to the Stockholm Concert Hall for the seventy-fifth Nobel Prize ceremony. In Sweden, close to the Arctic Circle, daylight is limited to four to five hours during December. The Concert Hall, its design inspired by classical Greek temples, is bright blue. From the darkness, the Friedmans entered the magnificent brightly lit, flower-adorned hall. More than a thousand dignitaries and distinguished guests were present—the women wearing colorful ball gowns; the men dressed in white tie and tails. Even Friedman's and Rose's bodyguards wore the formal black and white tuxedoes.

A blare of trumpets by the Stockholm Philharmonic Orchestra announced the arrival of King Carl and Queen Sylvia, along with their son Prince Bertil and his wife, Princess Lillian, at 5:00 PM. They were followed onto the historic stage by the laureates.

The long ceremony was filled with speeches extolling the virtues and significant contributions of the award winners. Musical selections were presented between every event on the program.

The prize in economics is always the last to be awarded. When it was Friedman's turn to be recognized and to receive his diploma and gold medal, he stood up from his chair and began his walk to the center of the stage to meet the king. Then, a heckler interrupted the presentation, yelling protests from the balcony. Immediately, security grabbed the formally attired protestor and escorted him out of the hall. Friedman and the king proceeded to center stage. Following custom, the king left the laureate to receive the audience's ovation. Friedman's ovation was longer than that of "any of the preceding six laureates," he would recall. At subsequent events, people apologized profusely to Friedman and Rose for the embarrassing interruption by the anti-Pinochet protestor.

Newspapers reported that more than 2,000 demonstrators were outside the Concert Hall the night of the ceremony. The guests were inconvenienced more than the Friedmans, however, because the couple was driven a back route to the Gold Room at City Hall for the grand Nobel banquet, bypassing the crowded streets. Approximately 1,300 specially invited guests, including 250 local students, attended the banquet. Multiple toasts and speeches were given between the dinner courses. The evening concluded with dancing and partying in the Blue Room. The Friedmans enjoyed a little dancing and a lot of talking with some of the university students.

On Saturday, Friedman and Rose attended a banquet at the Royal Palace hosted by the king and queen to honor the laureates. Men outnumbered women on this occasion, for many men from the Nobel Foundation

King Carl Gustaf of Sweden congratulates Friedman at the Nobel Prize ceremony, December 10, 1976.

had been invited but not their wives. Following dinner, each laureate met separately with the king and queen. Friedman had met King Carl previously, when the king had visited the University of Chicago in spring 1975. Also, the Friedmans spoke with Prince Bertil.

The Friedmans relaxed and enjoyed a leisurely drive in the countryside on Sunday. The traditional luncheon hosted by the Stockholm School of Economics to honor the recipient of the Nobel Memorial Prize in Economics was Monday. Following the meal, Friedman gave his Nobel lecture. According to the Nobel Prize committee, Milton Friedman had received the prize "for his achievements in the fields of consumption analysis, monetary history and theory and for his demonstration of the complexity of stabilization policy." But his lecture did not pertain to any of these achievements. Instead, he chose to explain why economics is a scientific discipline like physics or chemistry or medicine, and therefore should be included among the Nobel Prize awards, rather than a part of philosophy or politics, as some critics of the award had argued.

Later that night the Friedmans flew home to the United States to begin a new phase in their long partnership together. The couple moved into their new California home in January 1977, and within a few months Friedman started a new job at the Hoover Institution in Palo Alto. Herbert Hoover had founded the Hoover Institution on War, Revolution and Peace at his alma mater, Stanford University, in 1919, to employ respected scholars to study economic, political, and social changes in the United States.

Friedman delivers his Nobel speech. He joked that since the announcement of his award, people had been asking his opinion "on everything from a cure for the common cold to the market value of a letter signed by John F. Kennedy."

The Friedmans lived in a high-rise building with views of San Francisco Bay and Alcatraz Island, and Friedman commuted the thirty miles to his office two or three days a week. From Friedman's study in the apartment (his desk as messy as ever), he had a view of the city. He and Rose had been married now for thirty-eight years. Janet and her family lived nearby. Rose wrote, "Our life together has seen high spots and low spots but rarely dull spots. In general, the low spots came early, the high spots later."

One high spot occurred when Friedman received a telephone call from Robert "Bob" Chitester, chief executive officer of PBS television station WQLN in Erie, Pennsylvania. According to Friedman, it was "a telephone call that launched us on the most exciting venture of our lives." Chitester had some thoughts on how to spread free-market ideas that he wanted Friedman and Rose to consider. The Friedmans agreed to a meeting.

Chitester had many proposals to offer, including a television documentary. John Kenneth Galbraith already had starred in a television series on the history of economic thought. Galbraith—witty, brilliant, and tall (six feet, eight inches)—had been instrumental in introducing Keynesian economics to the masses. Also, he had been an influential advisor to Franklin Roosevelt and the New Deal. Friedman, thinking that a television series on free-market ideas would be a way to present a balanced ideology to the public, agreed to devote eighteen months to the project once Chitester obtained funding. In all, Friedman and Rose would devote about three years to the project.

10 Free to Choose

The television series Friedman and Rose developed with Bob Chitester was titled *Free to Choose*, and makes the case that people are better off when their government is restricted to a few basic functions, so that people are allowed more freedom to choose in accordance with their own preferences and circumstances. The documentary consisted of ten programs. Each program began with Milton Friedman speaking from various locales around the world on a specific subject, such as the Great Depression, Keynesianism, inflation, and government regulation. In each show's second half, Friedman and invited guests discussed the subject at hand in segments filmed at the University of Chicago. Friedman wanted a philosophically balanced discussion, and the invited guests included experts both for and against the free-market principles emphasized in the program.

Throughout the production, Friedman had final approval of the scripts, and Rose was involved in all aspects of the filming. To augment the television series, the Friedmans coauthored a *Free to Choose* book, published in 1979.

In January 1980, the first program was broadcasted on 72 percent of the PBS stations in the United States. It was estimated that the first episode reached an audience of about 3 million viewers. (The series was later broadcasted in other countries.) The majority of letters received from the public were positive, and both the book and the series were a personal and financial success. The book was number one on the best-selling nonfiction list in 1980.

The 1980 Republican candidate for president, Ronald Reagan, created an Economic Policy Coordinating Committee to begin advance planning for the legislative agenda to be initiated during the first one hundred days in office, should he win the election. There

Friedman was a tireless champion of free-market economics as well as individual liberty. In 1980 he brought this message to millions of television viewers with the PBS series *Free to Choose*.

were thirteen members on the committee, including Milton Friedman. George Shultz served as chairman. The committee members met to agree on what the new economic policy agenda would include. No one member of the committee wrote the lengthy agenda report. Instead, the report was divided into sections and each member assumed responsibility for writing one or more sections. Periodically, the committee members met to provide progress updates and to discuss strategy.

On election night, Rose and Friedman joined George Shultz and his wife to listen to the election returns. That same night, Friedman and Shultz finalized the "Economic Strategy for the Reagan Administration" agenda report. Reagan won, becoming the fortieth president on January 20, 1981. Friedman would later write that "Once in office, Reagan acted very much along the lines that we recommended."

President Reagan formed a President's Economic Policy Advisory Board consisting of twelve economists. Friedman was selected to serve as a member of the board; again, George Shultz served as the chairman. All members of the board shared a free-market philosophy, although they differed on certain issues, and, on occasion, with President Reagan. Neither Friedman nor any other member could be accused of always saying yes to the president.

The board met with Reagan six times the first year of his presidency. In preparation for each meeting, Chairman Shultz notified the board on the economic issues President Reagan wanted to discuss. Board members then shared the tasks of preparing a brief analysis

A meeting of President Ronald Reagan's Economic Policy Advisory Board. Friedman (left) is seated next to board chairman George P. Shultz; Schultz later served as Reagan's secretary of state.

of each issue to be discussed. On the day of the meeting with President Reagan, the board convened around 10:00 AM to clarify and discuss differences in opinions, and to agree on what to report. Around 11:00 AM, President Reagan, Vice President George H. W. Bush, Chief of Staff James Baker, and two or three other advisors joined the board of economic advisors. A spirited, open discussion often ensued with President Reagan actively involved.

"During the first several years, inflation, monetary policy, and tax policy were understandably frequent topics," Friedman later recalled. He found President Reagan well informed on the issues presented, and receptive to hearing the different views offered in the discussions. Friedman wrote, "No other president in my lifetime comes close to Reagan in adherence to clearly specified principles dedicated to promoting and maintaining a free society."

Friedman and Rose were happy being Californians, and they decided to sell their home in New England and purchase a second California home on a one-acre lot at Sea Ranch, a housing development about two and a half hours north of their apartment in San Francisco. Sea Ranch had been a sheep ranch; now it was a development with tennis courts, pool, golf course, restaurant, and a private security force for the homeowners to share. The scenic area of meadows and pine trees had hiking trails and lots of deer, and their house was situated on a bluff with a spectacular view of the Pacific Ocean—the distance between the ocean and the house about one-half mile. It took two years to renovate their house, which included doubling its size. They also added a greenhouse. Rose grew vegetables and planted a variety of colorful flowers around the property. Whenever possible, they entertained and hosted events for family and friends.

Janet and her husband had divorced, although she still lived in the San Francisco Bay area. She remarried on June 25, 1982, the day that her parents celebrated forty-four years of marriage. That same year, George Stigler was awarded the Nobel Memorial Prize in Economics "for his seminal studies of industrial structures, functioning of markets and causes and effects of public regulation," according to the Nobel Prize committee. A year later, on June 4, 1983, David remarried.

During President Reagan's second term in office, the Economic Policy Advisory Board met fewer times because the Reagan administration had become engrossed in more non-economic issues, such as the Iran-Contra affair. Despite less work in Washington, Friedman and Rose remained busy both personally and professionally. Friedman continued his work at the Hoover Institution, and he continued researching, writing, and public speaking. Rose was recognized for her contribution to economics when Pepperdine University presented her with an honorary doctorate.

The couple traveled to Louisiana in late 1984 on a trip that combined business and pleasure. Friedman gave a lecture in New Orleans, and they visited David, who was teaching at Tulane University, and his family. During the visit, Friedman suffered a heart attack, and he remained in a local hospital for two weeks recovering. Once he could travel, Friedman returned to California and had a second bypass operation at Stanford Hospital, located on the Stanford University campus. Fortunately, there were no complications following the surgery or significant repercussions from the attack, and the couple were soon back into their familiar routine.

On June 25, 1988, Friedman and Rose celebrated fifty years of marriage. The Friedman family—including Janet's and David's spouses and two of their grandchildren, Rick and Patri—spent two weeks vacationing in Ecuador and the Galapagos Islands to celebrate. There were two other major accomplishments that year: Friedman was awarded the National Medal of Science and the Presidential Medal of Freedom.

The National Medal of Science is awarded by the National Science Foundation to an individual who has

The Friedmans in China, 1988. That year, the couple celebrated fifty years of marriage.

made a significant contribution to knowledge in the physical, biological, mathematical, engineering, and social or behavioral sciences. According to the National Science Foundation, "The National Medal of Science is the nation's highest scientific honor." It was established by the United States Congress in 1959.

While the National Medal of Science honors scientists, the Presidential Medal of Freedom is the highest award the United States bestows on a civilian. American citizens from politicians to scientists to actors are eligible for the award: "Recipients of the medal are those who have made outstanding contributions to the security or national interest of the United States or to world peace, or those who have made a significant public or private accomplishment." President Reagan awarded the medal to Friedman on October 17, 1988, along with eight other recipients. Guests invited to the ceremony included two of Friedman's nephews, Rose, and grandson Patri.

A year later Friedman and Rose experienced the San Francisco Bay area's Loma Prieta earthquake on October 17, 1989. Part of a freeway in Oakland collapsed, trapping and killing motorists. Fires broke out in the Marina District when gas lines broke. The quake caused deep cracks in the Santa Cruz Mountains. The Friedmans' apartment building shook, although the earthquake caused no major damage to their building, other than knocking out the elevator service. Friedman and Rose walked up and down the steps to their apartment on the nineteenth floor until service was restored. Friedman was at the apartment during the earthquake, while Rose was at the dentist's office. Once again they considered themselves lucky.

In September 1991, George Stigler and Rose gave her brother Aaron Director a surprise party in honor of his ninetieth birthday. Former colleagues, students, relatives, and friends from all over the country met one summer evening at a home near Stanford University. Director, believing he was attending a dinner at the home of a friend, rode to the party with Friedman and Rose. When they escorted him to the backyard of the house, the honoree was surprised and excited to see so many of his friends at the party.

A few months later Friedman and Rose were in Europe to attend a celebration of the ninetieth Nobel awards ceremony when Gloria Valentine, Friedman's secretary, called to tell them some sad news. George

Stigler had died of a massive heart attack. Stigler and Friedman, friends for more than fifty years, had shared a love of bridge and a passion for economics. Both had received many accolades, including the Nobel Prize in Economics.

Still active and in good health, for the next few years the Friedmans enjoyed traveling as much for recreational purposes as for professional. They took cruises to Greece and Hong Kong. A bad back did not stop Friedman from cruising to New Zealand. Soon after a spinal laminectomy, he and Rose boarded the ship in San Francisco; to get around on deck, Friedman used a walker.

June 1997 marked the fiftieth anniversary of the Mont Pelerin Society. Only three out of the original thirty-nine members were still alive, including Friedman and his brother-in-law, Aaron Director, and only Friedman attended the anniversary meeting. He and Rose flew to Mont Pelerin, Switzerland. Although the number of attendees was limited for this special celebration, there were still too many people for the Hotel du Parc, and the conference was held at a larger resort hotel.

Friedman wrote, "The world had changed, yet the issues discussed fifty years earlier seemed entirely topical." Premier Mikhail Gorbachev of Soviet Russia, President Reagan of the United States, and Prime Minister Margaret Thatcher of England had succeeded in ending the Cold War. The Berlin Wall had come falling down in 1989. Many bragged that capitalism had triumphed. Still, to Friedman's dismay, governments had continued to get bigger and deficits larger. In his opinion, the threat to economic, political, and human

Ronald Reagan bestows on Friedman the Presidential Medal of Freedom, America's highest civilian award, 1988.

freedom was still a reality. Both Friedman and Rose would state that the economies of countries such as the United States were "less free than they were when the society was founded," primarily because total government spending and regulation had significantly increased. They would write that "The regulatory and welfare state, not the socialist state, became, and remains, the main threat to freedom."

The Friedmans were good friends with the Czech prime minister Vaclav Klaus, a free-market economist and member of the Mont Pelerin Society. Following the Mont Pelerin meeting, they flew to Prague, where Friedman gave lectures and held discussions with some government and business leaders. From Prague they traveled to London to attend a *Free to Choose* reunion. Twenty years had passed since the conception of a television series to spread the word of free-market ideas, and the Friedmans hosted a party to thank various people who had participated in the project.

Friedman and Rose decided to coauthor another book. *Two Lucky People* is about their lives. Published in 1998, it tells the story of a special partnership between two economists and their marriage of sixty years. They write of the momentous changes they had witnessed:

> The world at the end of our life is very different from the world in which we grew up—in some ways enormously better, in other ways, worse. Materially, the wonders of science and enterprise have greatly enriched the world—though some products of science, like atomic energy, have been a mixed blessing. Few monarchs of ancient times could have lived as well as we have.

In addition, they wrote about some of the negative changes they had witnessed, including a tremendous growth in the prison population and the size of governments.

In 2002, they sold their home at Sea Ranch. The couple was traveling less, although they did make a trip that year to Washington, D.C. The Cato Institute—a think-tank promoting free-market principles—had created the Milton Friedman Prize for Advancing Liberty, and the Friedmans attended the inaugural ceremony. (The $500,000 award is given every other year.) While in Washington, ninety-year-old Friedman and ninety-one-year-old Rose attended a lunch at the White House, where President George W. Bush honored Friedman for his work on behalf of liberty.

Rose lost her beloved brother, and Friedman his close friend, when Aaron died at the age of 102 on September 11, 2004. Out of the original group of Chicago economists, only Rose and Friedman were left. They had their children and grandkids, though. Janet and David both lived in California now, and there were the four grandchildren: Janet's son Rick Stansby; and David's children, Patri, Becca, and William.

Friedman and Rose did not travel much, and Friedman had long ago ceased to play tennis or hike in the mountains, but he continued writing and speaking. The Friedmans remained actively involved in their foundation for promoting vouchers in education. Friedman gave talks via satellite; he continued researching and writing. He did not permit his failing eyesight to impede his curiosity and interest in economics and politics. He kept current with national and world events. He also maintained ties to the Hoover Institution, where employees collected and forwarded his mail.

Friedman contracted a serious viral infection and was admitted to the hospital in fall 2006. After a few days he returned home, where he died of congestive heart failure on November 16 at the age of ninety-four. His body was cremated. A memorial service was held at the University of Chicago on January 29, 2007. The distinguished guests invited to speak at the service included the professor's former student, Gary Becker (1992 Nobel laureate) and Vaclav Klaus, president of the Czech Republic, a country that had once been communist, but is now free.

Milton and Rose Friedman, married for 68 years, were partners in every sense of the word. "Our life has surpassed our wildest expectations," they wrote in their 1998 memoir, *Two Lucky People*.

Klaus recalled growing up in a communist country, and what an important influence Friedman had been on him, presenting a theory and world view so different than the one Klaus encountered in his daily life. As such, Klaus allied with Friedman and the Chicago school of economic thought. Though he didn't know Friedman as well as some of the other speakers at the memorial, his speech summed up Friedman's life and contributions: "We all admired him for the clarity of his thinking as well as for his intellectual stubbornness and —at the same time—for his personal kindness and charm. Nothing expresses his life better than the title of the book he wrote together with Rose: *Two Lucky People*. From what I know, I can confirm that they were lucky, that they were lucky together and I would add that we were lucky to have had Milton Friedman."

Time Line

1912: Milton Friedman born July 31 in Brooklyn, New York.

1917: Begins school.

1928: Enrolls in Rutgers University.

1932: Begins graduate studies at the University of Chicago.

1935: Moves to Washington, D.C., as an economist in Roosevelt's New Deal.

1937: Takes a job at National Bureau of Economic Research in New York.

1938: Marries Rose Director on June 25.

1940: Becomes visiting professor at the University of Wisconsin.

1941: Works at Treasury in Washington, D.C.

1946: Returns to the University of Chicago as professor of economics.

1947: Attends inaugural meeting of the Mont Pelerin Society in Switzerland.

1957: Publishes *A Theory of the Consumption Function*.

1962: Publishes the popular *Capitalism & Freedom*.

1963: Publishes *A Monetary History of the United States*.

1966: Becomes columnist for *Newsweek* magazine.

1976: Receives Nobel Memorial Prize in Economics.

1977: Moves to San Francisco and works at the Hoover Institution.

1979: *Free to Choose* published and the series televised.

1988: Receives the National Medal of Science and Presidential Medal of Freedom.

2006: Dies November 16 in San Francisco, California.

Source Notes

1: Early Years

p. 6, "When they arrived . . ." Milton Friedman and Rose Friedman, *Free to Choose* (San Diego: Harcourt, Inc., 1980), 1.

p. 12, "musical illiterate." Milton Friedman and Rose D. Friedman, *Two Lucky People* (Chicago: The University of Chicago Press, 1998), 21.

p. 16, "was in college not . . ." Ibid., 25.

p. 22, "I cannot say I took . . ." Ibid., 33.

2: Capitalism at Risk

p. 24, "Controversies among faculty members . . ." Friedman and Friedman, *Two Lucky People*, 35.

p. 27, "caused by excesses . . ." Lanny Ebenstein, *Milton Friedman* (New York: Palgrave Macmillan, 2007), 114.

p. 29, "On the contrary . . ." R. F. Harrod, *The Life of John Maynard Keynes* (London: MacMillan & Co., Ltd., 1952), 405.

p. 31, "refused to cooperate," Friedman and Friedman, *Two Lucky People*, 42.

p. 34, "economics, economics, economics," Ibid., 54.

3: Petty Politics

p. 37, "the consumption function . . ." Ebenstein, *Milton Friedman*, 36.

p. 38, "We had the feeling . . ." Friedman and Friedman, *Two Lucky People*, 60-61.

p. 40, "It was never a question . . ." Ibid., 84.

p. 43, "born under a lucky star." Ibid., 89.

p. 44, "home was always open . . ." Ibid., 93.

p. 45, "a pawn in an internal . . ." Ibid., 102.

p. 45, "As I look back . . ." Ibid., 104.

p. 46, "I came to understand . . ." Ibid., 110.

p. 48, "thoroughly Keynesian." Ibid., 113.

p. 50, "It is far easier . . ." Ibid., 123.

p. 50, "by all means . . ." Ibid., 110.

4: Professor Friedman

p. 53, "lived, breathed, and slept . . ." Friedman and Friedman, *Two Lucky People*, 149.

p. 57, "thoroughly Keynesian." Ibid., 113.

p. 58, "Time and again . . ." Ibid., 204.

p. 61, "to halt and reverse . . ." R. M. Hartwell, *A History of the Mont Pelerin Society* (Indianapolis: Liberty Fund, 1995), 34.

p. 63, "mainly for the benefit . . ." Ibid., xiii.

5: Travel and Theory

p. 66, "My interest in public policy . . ." Friedman and Friedman, *Two Lucky People*, 333.

p. 72, "he made a suggestion," Ibid., 266.

p. 72, "tracing the evolution . . ." Ebenstein, *Milton Friedman*, 117.

p. 74, "got a shower . . ." Friedman and Friedman, *Two Lucky People*, 276.

6: Great Books

p. 77, "The total stock . . ." Milton Friedman and Anna Jacobson Schwartz, *A Monetary History of the United States 1867–1960* (Princeton: Princeton University Press, 1963), 352.

p. 78, "Far from the depression . . ." Friedman and Friedman, *Two Lucky People*, 233.

p. 80, "The appropriate free market . . ." Milton Friedman, *Capitalism & Freedom* (Chicago: The University of Chicago Press, 1962), 36.

p. 81, "Competition would force . . ." Friedman and Friedman, *Two Lucky People*, 349.

p. 81, "To Janet and David . . ." Friedman, *Capitalism & Freedom*, dedication page.

7: Wanderjahr

p. 82, "favorite pastime in Paris," Friedman and Friedman, *Two Lucky People*, 280.

p. 83, "first real introduction . . ." Ibid., 281.

p. 83, "looked around the room . . ." Ibid.

p. 85, "were a state secret." Ibid., 285.

p. 86, "Though we were not . . ." Ibid., 295–296.

p. 87, "sharply different political . . ." Ibid., 305.

p. 88, "On every side . . ." Ibid., 315.

p. 89, "nearly a tenth . . ." Ibid., 312.

p. 90, "seemed like an American . . ." Ibid., 316.

p. 91, "a shoppers' . . ." Ibid.

p. 91, "rated first," Ibid., 318.

8: Public Figure

p. 94, "Inflation is always . . ." Milton Friedman, *An Economist's Protest* (Glen Ridge: Thomas Horton and Company, 1972), 29.

p. 95, "a heretic . . ." Lanny Ebenstein, *Milton Friedman*, 138.

p. 99,   "the age of . . ." Ibid., 105.

p. 100, "research findings were barren . . ." Friedman and
         Friedman, *Two Lucky People*, 356.

p. 102, "No public-policy . . ." Ibid., 381.

p. 102, "Friedman is a man . . ." "The Intellectual Provocateur,"
         Time (December 19, 1969),
         http://www.time.com/time/printout/0,8816,941753,00.html.

p. 107, "The key economic problems . . ." Friedman and
         Friedman, *Two Lucky People*, 591.

p. 107, "a fascist military junta that . . ." Ibid., 402.

9: Nobel Laureate

p. 114, "any of the preceding . . ." Friedman and Friedman, *Two
         Lucky People*, 452.

p. 115, "for his achievements . . ." Nobel Prize Organization, *The
         Sveriges Riksbank Prize in Economic Sciences in Memory of
         Alfred Nobel 1976*, http://nobelprize.org/nobel_prizes/
         economics/laureates/1976.

p. 116, "on everything from . . ." Milton Friedman, speech at the
         Nobel banquet (December 10, 1976).
         http://nobelprize.org/nobel_prizes/economics/
         laureates/1976/friedman-speech.html

p. 117, "Our life together . . ." Friedman and Friedman, *Two
         Lucky People*, 409.

p. 117, "a telephone call that . . ." Ibid., 471.

10: Free to Choose

p. 120, "Once in office . . ." Friedman and Friedman, *Two Lucky
         People*, 390.

p. 121, "During the first several years . . ." Ibid., 393.

p. 121, "No other president . . ." Ibid., 396.

p. 122, "for his seminal studies . . ." Nobel Prize Organization, *The Sveriges Riksbank Prize in Economic Sciences in Memory of Alfred Nobel 1982*, http://nobelprize.org/nobel_prizes/economics/laureates/1982.

p. 124, "The National Medal of . . ." National Science Foundation, http://www.nsf.gov/news/news_summ.jsp?cntn_id=100684.

p. 124, "Recipients of the medal . . ." Presidential Medal of Freedom, http://www.medaloffreedom.com.

p. 126, "The world had changed . . ." Friedman and Friedman, *Two Lucky People*, 582.

p. 127, "less free than they were . . ." Ibid., 583.

p. 127, "The regulatory and . . ." Ibid., 582.

p. 128, "The world at the end . . ." Ibid., 587.

p. 130, "We all admired him . . ." Vaclav Klaus, "Remarks at Milton Friedman's funeral service," http://www.hrad.cz/cms/en/prezident_cr/klaus_projevy/4259.shtml.

Bibliography

Barro, Robert J., Bruce Caldwell, Lee A. Coppock, Donald J. Devine, Richard M. Ebeling, Steve Forbes, Lord Robert Skidelsky, and Mark Skousen. *Great Economists of the Twentieth Century*. Hillsdale: Hillsdale College Press, 2006.

Biven, W. Carl. *Who Killed John Maynard Keynes?* Homewood: Dow Jones-Irwin, 1989.

Buchanan, James M., and Richard E. Wagner. *Democracy in Deficit: The Political Legacy of Lord Keynes*. Orlando: Academic Press, Inc., 1977.

Ebeling, Richard M., and Sheldon Richman. "Milton Friedman (1912–2006)." *The Freeman*, Vol. 56, No. 10 (December 2006): 31–33.

Ebenstein, Alan. *Friedrich Hayek: A Biography*. Chicago: The University of Chicago Press, 2003.

Ebenstein, Lanny. *Milton Friedman*. New York: Palgrave Macmillan, 2007.

Frazer, William. *The Legacy of Keynes and Friedman*. Westport: Praeger Publishers, 1994.

Free to Choose Enterprise. *Free to Choose* (1980). http://www.free-tochoose.net

Friedman, Milton. *Capitalism & Freedom*. Chicago: The University of Chicago Press, 1962.

———. "Economists and Economic Policy." *Economic Inquiry*, Vol. 24, No. 1 (January 1986): 1–10.

———. *An Economist's Protest*. Glen Ridge: Thomas Horton and Company, 1972.

———. "The Role of Monetary Policy." *The American Economic Review*, Vol. 58, No. 1 (March 1968): 1–17.

———. *A Theory of the Consumption Function*. Princeton: Princeton University Press for the National Bureau of Economic Research, 1957

Friedman, Milton and Rose Friedman. *Free to Choose: A Personal Statement*. San Diego: A Harvest Book, Harcourt, Inc., 1980.

———. *Two Lucky People*. Chicago: The University of Chicago Press, 1998.

Friedman, Milton and Anna Jacobson Schwartz. *A Monetary History of the United States 1867–1960*. Princeton: Princeton University Press for the National Bureau of Economic Research, 1963.

Harrod, R. F. *The Life of John Maynard Keynes*. London: MacMillan & Co., Ltd., 1952.

Hartwell, R. M. *A History of the Mont Pelerin Society*. Indianapolis: Liberty Fund, 1995.

Hayek, Friedrich. *The Road to Serfdom*. Chicago: The University of Chicago Press, 1944.

Henderson, David. "Biography of Friedrich August Hayek (1899–1992)." Liberty Fund, The Library of Economics and Liberty, http://www.econlib.org/library/Enc/bios/Hayek.html.

The Idea Channel. *The Power of Choice: The Life and Ideas of Milton Friedman* (2007). http://www.ideachannel.com

"The Intellectual Provocateur." *Time* (December 19, 1969), http://www.time.com/time/printout/0,8816,941753,00.html.

National Science Foundation. http://www.nsf.gov

Nobel Prize Organization. http://nobelprize.org/nobel_prizes/economics/laureates

The Presidential Medal of Freedom. http://medaloffreedom.com.

Rogge, Benjamin A. *Can Capitalism Survive?* Indiana: Liberty Fund, The Library of Economics and Liberty, http://www.econlib.org/library/LFBooks/Rogge/rggCCS3.html.

Samuelson, Robert J. "Great Depression." Liberty Fund, The Library of Economics and Liberty, http://www.econlib.org/library/Enc/Great Depression.

"Special Report: Milton Friedman." *The Economist*, Vol. 381, No. 8505 (November 25–December 1, 2006): 79–80.

Websites

http://www.nobelprize.org/nobel_prizes/economics/
laureates/1976/friedman-autobio.html

> The Web site of the Nobel Foundation features Milton Friedman's autobiography, his Nobel Prize lecture, and banquet speech, along with links to other sources.

http://www.friedmanfoundation.org

> The Friedman Foundation for Educational Choice provides short biographies of Milton and Rose Friedman on this site, as well as links to his writings on school choice.

http://www.hoover.org/bios/friedman.html

> Friedman was a senior fellow at the Hoover Institution at Stanford University from 1977 to 2006, and this site has links to a short biography of Friedman and his publications, including a transcript of a filmed interview on "Economics and War: The Economic Impact of the War on Terrorism."

http://www.achievement.org/autodoc/page/fri0gal-1

> One of the best features of The Academy of Achievement's page on Milton Friedman is its link to an interview with Friedman on January 31, 1991. Visitors to the site can read a transcript of the interview, watch a video of it, or listen to an audio. The site also has a profile, biography, and photo gallery of Friedman.

http://www.pbs.org/wgbh/commandingheights/shared/
minitextlo/int_miltonfriedman.html

> On January 31, 2000, PBS broadcast an interview with Milton Friedman during which he spoke on a range of topics: the Great Depression, the economic logic behind black markets, and his role in Chile under Pinochet. Read a transcript of this interview on this site, or watch a video.

Index

Numbers in **bold italics** refer to captions.

Picture Credits